A Jack Rabbit Novel

The Lawrence County Moonshine War

I0584036

Earl Snort

White Glove Fiction Series: Book Three

White Glove Fiction
1103 Middlecreek
Friendswood, Texas 77546
281-992-3131 281-482-5390 Fax
www.WhiteGloveFiction.com

Copyright © 2022 by Earl Snort

ISBN: 978-1-64883-1249
UPC: 6-43977-41249-2

FIRST EDITION
1   2   3   4   5   6   7   8   9   10

Not a speck of this is true. It's all a pack of lies.

This tale is dedicated to ZAB and CWB, members of the younger generation whom I love with all my heart. Not that many years down the road, the destiny of America will rest upon their shoulders, and upon the shoulders of millions of other Americans who were born during the same decade or so. God bless them all. God Bless America.

Earl Snort - 2021

Table of Contents

In Memoriam

This tale is in memory and honor of CBB. He was born in the last decade of the 19th century, the son of a farmer, and the grandson and great-nephew of five Confederate veterans. His middle name was in honor of a three-time populist Democrat nominee for President who never attained the Oval Office. CBB was a Christian first, and subsequently a farmer, soldier, migrant orange picker, and a factory worker by trade.

He enlisted in the Army during the Great War, serving in France. This was the first time he had been more than twenty miles from the site of his nativity. He nearly lost his life in France but not from an enemy bullet. He sustained a severe cut which resulted in a nearly fatal case of tetanus. The Army physician feared it would turn to gangrene and wanted to amputate his arm as a lifesaving measure. CBB begged him not to. He didn't, and CBB barely pulled through. Later, towards the end of the war, he caught dysentery. This big, strapping farm boy was only a shadow of his former self when he was honorably discharged as a corporal after thirteen months of service.

He returned home to the family farm. His health and his life improved substantially. He married his sweetheart. Then one night the barn caught fire, which spread to the house. Everything but human life was lost. They had no insurance. They sold the land to pay off debts.

His family packed all they had into a Model T Ford and drove to Florida, where they picked oranges as migrant workers. They remained two years until his bride became pregnant. They returned to their home county. CBB found employment in a factory which manufactured automobile parts as a drill press operator.

During the next fifteen years, CBB and his wife had five children, one of whom perished in infancy.

In 1929, the Great Depression came knocking with a vengeance. CBB was laid off work for seven years. Nevertheless, each weekday he walked three miles to the factory. Some days he got picked up as spot labor. Other days he walked back home empty-handed.

To survive, CBB's widowed mother took in laundry, starching and ironing white shirts for college students and office workers. His wife cleaned houses. The two older sons mowed yards, shoveled coal, delivered newspapers, and any other odd job they could find. The family grew a two-acre garden each summer. CBB hunted for game during hunting season.

The family also helped out at CBB's in-laws' farm on Saturdays. In return, they were given vegetables and fruit which they canned, eggs and milk if there were a surplus, and the occasional live chicken to butcher for a Sunday meal. Each November they butchered a hog. They rationed the meat because it had to last until the following November.

If they earned at least ten dollars a week, they could limp by until the following week. Ten dollars was enough to pay the interest on the home mortgage, the light bill, coal, a gallon of gas for the Model T, a few store-bought commodities, and other necessities.

When they were completely tapped out, CBB's sister and her husband, who owned a small corner grocery, would give them credit for commodities and other things they needed. Throughout all those years, CBB maintained a running tab with them. His brother-in-law's good will kept the wolves off CBB's doorstep and he was thankful.

Finally, in 1937, the economy began to turn around. CBB went back to work. Both sons found regular part-time employment after school. The family began to enjoy a degree of prosperity. FDR was their savior who, besides the Lord, received all the credit.

In 1941, World War Two was thrust upon America "on a date that will live in infamy." The factory began working many hours of overtime for wartime production. Money problems began to fade away. Two sons went into the Army. One went to Europe and the other went to the Pacific.

After the war, CBB sold their home in town and purchased twenty acres with a ramshackle farmhouse in the vicinity of his family's old homestead. He made the home improvements himself and remained there in contentment for the rest of his days. Life had turned full circle for him, from prosperity to poverty and back to prosperity again, although he still endured hardships just like we all do until we are called Home.

He was an old man when he passed away - three score and ten plus some. It is interesting to note that CBB never lived in a house with a flush toilet. He always used an outhouse. His widow spent a portion of his life insurance money to put in a modern bathroom with a sink, bathtub, and flush toilet.

CBB was the most honest, forthright, kindest, man I ever knew. He was a tower of strength, both physically and in terms of character. He was a Sunday school superintendent for twelve years. He was a lifelong fan of his high school basketball team and the Chicago Cubs, the former of which he always managed to maintain one season ticket, even throughout the Depression, and the latter of which he faithfully listened to on the radio if he wasn't working. (In those days the Cubs only played day games.)

CBB loved cigars. We always gave him a box of his favorite brand for Christmas and his birthday. He kept a bottle of bourbon stashed in a kitchen cabinet. It was only uncorked and consumed for medicinal purposes, or so I was told. (I never saw him drink a drop so it was probably true.) He subscribed to *Grit*, "America's Greatest Family Newspaper." It was published weekly. I always loved reading it.

He owned about a half-dozen rifles and shotguns. The rifles were all .22 caliber and the shotguns were all 12-gauge. All but one gun, a rifle, were single shots as I recall. Years later he got a new pump shotgun as a gift when he retired from the factory. He kept all his guns in the kitchen in the corner next to the hutch. The ammo was in the top hutch drawer. In those days nobody was afraid that an unauthorized person might steal one and massacre the whole family or even the neighborhood. Folks never locked their houses or their automobiles. What a different world we live in today!

CBB loved horses, particularly draft horses, because he had plowed with them (mostly Belgians) all his life. In 1948, his youngest son finally convinced him to buy a Farmall tractor. It allowed them to plow the fields in a quarter of the time. It made his son very happy.

CBB loved fried chicken, biscuits, roasting ears, hand-cranked ice cream, and watermelon. Especially watermelon. He grew his own. Remembering his youth, he always maintained that the best watermelon was a stolen watermelon. If it wasn't sweet, he'd bust it and feed it to the cows. His cows loved him.

He hated gambling in any format. That included playing

cards just for fun, even games like Rook. He maintained that gambling was the Devil's workshop.

This sums up CBB as best I can. He was my one and only true life hero. I have a photograph of him in his doughboy uniform hanging on the wall of my living room. I also have his honorable discharge certificate. I still miss him dearly after all these decades. I wish my wife and my son and my grandchildren could have known him.

I think he would have enjoyed this tale.

Earl Snort
2021

PREFACE

An Introduction to the Fantasy Aspect of This Tale

It was a great morning, bright, hot, and sunny in the West Texas hill country. Jack Rabbit was awake, moving away from his burrow, ready for breakfast. He was in the mood for some fresh sprouts and he knew exactly where they were growing up on the hillside. Jack weaved around the cactus and sage brush, starting up the well-known path to higher ground.

After a few minutes he paused, wondering what that sound was. Moving slow, he hopped closer to see. From behind a giant, red barrel cactus, he nosed around for a peek. To Jack's surprise, an Apache medicine man was chanting and dancing around a small fire. The medicine man was dressed in feathers and his body was painted in many colors. Most noticeable was his left hand. It was painted all white up to his wrist like a glove. In his right hand, he held what appeared to be a ball consisting of stones, sticks, feathers, cloth, and who knows what else wrapped around something which resembled a skull.

Jack heard a small crack and looked up the hillside. A small puff of dust spit out into the sunshine. Jack had seen rock slides before but this was different. He noticed a huge boulder vibrating and beginning to move. He was scared he would be in its path when it came tumbling down. Jack jumped sideways as rabbits do, and bolted. He let out a loud screech, screaming past the dancing medicine man. Shocked out of his trance, the shaman fell backwards into a crevice of the hillside.

Jack had seen the boulder start to fall, so he jumped into the narrow opening to get away from its path. Both Jack and the shaman watched as this very large rock bounced on the trail, falling over the side of the cliff. Without a doubt, Jack had saved the shaman's life.

The shaman looked down at Jack. "Wow! That was close. Thank you for saving my life. What's your name?"

"Jack Rabbit," replied the rabbit.

"Hello, Jack. My name is Mohan. I'm the medicine man for my Apache tribe."

"How do you speak my language?" asked Jack. "How is it I can understand you?"

"My God has empowered me with great wisdom and the ability to perform many wonderous tasks. May I ask you what you desire?"

Jack knew immediately what he wanted. "Currently my life is short compared to yours. I wish to be many things, to go many places, and to have a very long life."

Mohan climbed out of the crevice and rebuilt the fire. Jack remained in the crevice away from danger. Oncet the fire was just the right size, Mohan returned and went way back, deep into the darkness, mumbling words Jack could not understand. Jack could hear Mohan moving about, tapping and scraping in the dark. Jack jumped when Mohan let out a loud, "Ah ha! Found it!" and shuffled out of the recess. Back to the fire went Mohan, opening his medicine bag along the way. He pulled out several items and began to chant, repeating a rhythmic phrase, and dancing around the fire. After a few minutes, he called for Jack to come out of the crevice.

Cautiously, Jack crept out. He positioned himself close to Mohan, staying away from the cliff side and the fire. He was afraid to get too close to the fire because his fur could burn.

Mohan, still chanting and dancing, threw something into the flames which exploded. Jack jumped farther back, closer to the side of the hill. Mohan laughed and directed Jack to a specific spot. He motioned for Jack to move onto the top of a rock he had placed close to the fire.

Jack was hesitant but decided it would be safe with Mohan. He was nice and had a good voice for chanting.

Mohan stopped suddenly in front of Jack, throwing a dust ball towards him. Jack had been facing Mohan and now both his eyes and ears were filled with powder. In fact, the powder covered Jack from his head all the way down to his lucky feet. Rabbits have lucky feet, you know.

Mohan started to chant and to dance once again. The rhythmic sounds along with his hypnotic voice mesmerized Jack, causing him to sway back and forth.

Magical powers swirled all around them. Sparks flew from the fire. Clouds rolled in. Lightning lit up the sky. Rocks crashed down from the hill. Thunder rolled through the valley. Cacti burst into flowers. Grass turned emerald green. Water sprung from the crevice, forming a small creek which pursued gravity down the side of the hill. A star fell. All kinds of strange things happened as Mohan performed his magic spell.

Jack awoke feeling a little strange. Looking around, he saw Mohan sleeping on the ground next to the dying fire. Getting up, Jack hopped down to the creek to get a drink. The water was the sweetest he had ever tasted. Looking some more, he spotted some fresh, green, tender sprouts. They tasted really awesome. When he was sated, he hopped over to Mohan, who had just begun to rouse.

"What just happened?" asked Jack.

Mohan sat up and stretched. "Well, Jack," he said, "you are now a very special being. You have many powers to experiment with. First, let's test your abilities. Picture in your mind that you are an Apache warrior."

Jack thought, "I am an Apache warrior." The air stood still. A little fire flashed before his eyes. A wind blew in his face, producing a tear.

Mohan said, "Jack, go look at the reflection of your face in the stream."

Moving to the stream, Jack peered into the standing pool and saw an Apache warrior looking back at him. "Mohan," he cried. "What is going on?"

Mohan laughed a little and replied, "Jack, you are now what we call a changeling. A changeling is a being with many powers. Changelings can become anything they wish to be. Also, the spirits have granted you never-ending life. That means you can live forever. In addition, you have the power of time. You can venture to the past or the future; however, there is one catch to this magical existence. You can do no harm to others, except to the bad when they are harming others. Your life is now designed to be helpful to all beings wherever you go. Protect the innocent from the bad. This means you can use force when necessary."

Mohan paused. "Jack, there are two restrictions. You may never visit Easter Island, as the awful 'Z Gods' there will harm you. Also, you may never eat papaya fruit."

Jack wondered, "What is papaya fruit?" He didn't have a clue. Nevertheless, he didn't ask.

Over the next several weeks, Jack changed from one being to another - panther, eagle, mouse, etc. "This is amazing," he thought.

Jack wandered all over Apache territory for many years, changing however he saw fit. He thoroughly enjoyed being a bird. Birds can see many things on the ground in great detail. They fly fast and they travel long distances. He also liked being a ground animal. Being a panther was his favorite. Most of all, Jack liked being human, although he could be a big tree or a small bush when all he wanted to do was watch the world go by.

Jack traveled all over the world through time and space for the next hundred years, getting to experience all kinds of people, places, and things.

This tale is about just one of his adventures - one he especially enjoyed.

Chapter 1:
A New Awakening

Jack awoke with a start. It was early morning. The weather was crisp, a little frosty even. He smelled wood smoke in the air. When Jack dozed off the night before, he was near a dry creek bed in Apache County in West Texas. The weather had been blazing hot and dry with no humidity. He had been sweltering and thirsty. The scrub brush around him had been wind-blown, parched, and tasteless. He had lain awake until the wee hours of the night, watching a thousand stars twinkling overhead. He wished for a change of scenery, something not so dry or scorching - a place of his own. That's the last thing he remembered except for his name. He was a little chilled. Where in the world was he?

He sat up with a bolt. He had been lying on dewy green grass in a glen, surrounded by hardwood trees which reached to the sky from some decent-sized hills all around him. The trees were mostly oak, with a few sycamores, some gnarly cedars, and a smattering of maple, poplar, hickory, redbuds, dogwoods, and black walnut. The trees were covered with buds and young shoots. It must be spring, but where? Certainly not Apache County, Texas. Guess he got his wish. He was wrapped in an olive drab (OD), wool blanket. He could see US stenciled on the front. That's when it occurred to him that he was no longer a rabbit. He was a man, a soldier, all fitted out in olive drab outer garments, wearing wool breeches with leggings wrapped around his calves all the way down to his brown, ankle-high boots. He was wearing an OD military tunic with a high collar, over a white long-sleeve shirt. The tunic had black metal buttons and black, circular pins on each side of the collar. The pin on his right was marked US. The one on the left had crossed rifles, the nearly universal symbol of infantry.

Two chevrons were sown about three inches above the bottom on the left sleeve, and one was sown in the same location on the right sleeve. He didn't know what these chevrons represented when he woke up, but he learned later that the two on the left represented six months of overseas service each, and the one on the right represented a wound received in action. He didn't have any insignia on his shoulder straps, indicating that he was not an officer. Likewise, he did not have any chevrons in the middle of his sleeves, indicating that he was a private, the lowest rank in the Army, like half of the other soldiers who were honorably discharged from the U.S. Army during the Great War.

He also had a multicolored ribbon (purple, blue, green, yellow, red, yellow, green, blue, and purple, in blended vertical stripes) sown above his left breast pocket, and a diamond-shaped patch with a yellow eagle flying through a yellow circle sown above his right breast pocket. Finally, he had a red numeral one sown on the shoulder of his left sleeve. These were all mysteries as well, but the same person who explained the significance of the chevrons also explained that the red numeral one represented the 1st Infantry Division. The multicolored ribbon was awarded to veterans of the Allied Forces during Great War. The eagle was an emblem awarded to honorably discharged veterans, so the public would know they were no longer on active duty. The reasoning behind the 'ruptured duck' was because oftentimes veterans had no other clothing, nor the money to purchase new clothes when they were discharged, so they wore their uniforms until they could afford to buy some civvies.

Lying on the ground next to his blanket were his campaign (Smokey the Bear) hat and a canvas duck, military issue valise (personal kit) with a single, adjustable cross-shoulder strap. He unbuckled the leather straps on the flap and peaked inside. It contained a comb, razor, bar of soap, hand towel, toothbrush, a pair of folded documents, a pair of circular dog tags on a leather neck thong, two pairs of socks, small compass, foil-wrapped hardtack, brass padlock with two keys, a small New Testament, tin cup, small whetstone, tin mess kit including spoon, fork, and butter knife, thin brass box containing kitchen matches, small ball of string, small tablet, two pencils, a pair of undergarments, and a small cardboard box. He opened the box and looked inside. It contained a medal hanging on a ribbon the same color as the one stitched on his tunic. Not much stuff, if these were all his worldly possessions.

Then he looked at the folded documents. One was his honorable discharge certificate with his service record printed on the back. The other was an excerpt from an after-action report, in which he was "mentioned in dispatch" for dragging three wounded soldiers behind a large boulder, saving their lives while he was under enemy fire. He wondered whatever became of them. He put the documents and the boxed medal back into his valise.

He checked his pockets. Handkerchief, leather wallet with six one-dollar bills, a Louisville and Nashville (L&N) train ticket stub, and a photograph of an attractive young woman signed "Love, Phoebe." He also found a four-inch, single, locking-blade,

Case XX folding knife, a silver Ball railroad pocket watch with a broken mainspring on a woven leather chain, and a small drawstring leather pouch containing two double eagles, one single eagle, four silver dollars, three half-dollars, two quarters, four dimes, two nickels, and eight pennies. At least he wasn't broke. Another pocket contained a pouch of King Edward smoking tobacco, a well-used pipe, and a small box of matches. The last pocket contained an empty, eight-ounce, silver flask. He opened the lid and smelled the aroma of bourbon. Then he returned the flask back to where he found it. Much better.

Nonetheless, all of this was bewildering in that, at this very moment, all he could deduce was that he was a soldier in a moderate climate, location hopefully in the U.S., date unknown, and that he was ravenous. His stomach was touching his backbone. He stood up, brushed off his blanket, and rolled it up. He used a piece of rope that he found laying next to his valise to bind the blanket into a 'sausage roll' near each end to hold it in place and to fashion a sling.

He put on his hat. He looked around and walked over to the nearest tree to make water. Instant relief! He heard and then noticed a shallow, bubbling creek about twenty feet away. The water looked inviting. He retrieved the cup from his bag, and walked over to splash water on his face and to get a drink. He dipped the cup into the creek and had a sip. He savored the result. It was clear, cold, and without taste. No wonder. The stones in the water were limestone! What folks in West Texas wouldn't give for water this pure and cold! He drank to his heart's content.

Thirst quenched, he slung his blanket crossways across his left shoulder, akin to the way Confederate soldiers slung their bedrolls in a bygone generation. Then he slung his valise across his right shoulder. Time to press on. He began walking in the direction of the wood smoke in search of people. Pray to God he wasn't a deserter, or a criminal, or in enemy territory because he was unarmed. He felt naked without a firearm - any type of firearm - with ample ammunition, of course. Experience had taught him that mankind was not necessarily friendly, helpful, or benign.

He followed the smoke out of the glen into the woods and up to the top of a low ridge. A pleasant-looking log cabin with a wide, covered front verandah facing East was situated at the top. A barn and three other outbuildings were also in the curtilage. He saw a man about his own age, 25 perhaps, chopping kindling. The man paused to take Jack's measure. A yellow cur dog on the verandah sat up, alert but silent. He was watching Jack carefully. Jack decided that it was a good day to be a human and not a hare.

Jack approached to within fifteen feet of the man and stopped. He smiled, waived, and said, "Hello, the house."

The wood chopper left his axe blade buried in the block. He stood up erect and said, "Hello, yourself."

Jack noticed that they were both the same size - about five feet, nine inches tall, roughly a hundred and forty pounds, and similar in appearance - blue eyes, and short brown hair, except Jack had a thick mustache and the wood chopper was clean shaven. The wood chopper was dressed in a gray slouch hat, faded blue bib overalls, a white shirt with the sleeves rolled up just below the elbows, a red bandanna tied around his neck, and rundown, scuffed, brown boon dockers.

Jack said, "I don't mean to bother you, Mister. My name is John Archibald Rabbit. My friends call me Jack. It sounds crazy, but I'm completely lost. It appears that I'm suffering a loss of memory. I'm not sure how I got here other than to say I must have walked. I don't know where I am. I hope I'm not trespassing. If you can point me in the right direction, I'll be on my way."

"What's the right direction? What exactly are you looking for?"

"I don't know. I can't remember. Sorry. Maybe a town where I can get something to eat."

"Jack, for heaven's sake! Don't you recognize me? I'm your kin, Cousin Gerard Silas Twyman. You're standing right above Rabbit Holler where you just come from.

"Turn around. Take a gander. What you see in the foreground is all that's left of your grandpappy's place - twelve acres out of 160. All the buildings are gone! Burnt down! Struck by lightnin' in the midst of a big blow which spread the fire to all the buildings whilst you was off fightin' the war. Your grandpappy, pappy, and momma was all kilt. Burnt up. It was awful. We buried them in the family plot."

"Oh my! I didn't know."

"Oh my is right! After your folks passed, your sister sold all the property to Mr. Elias MacEwen. That's Mr. Mac to most ever'one hereabouts, exceptin' for them twelve acres down yonder.

"Jack, afore you say nary a word, she didn't have no choice! Your pappy owed too much money to Mr. Mac on account of all them horses he bought on credit what got burnt up in the barn, not to mention the whole season's worth of burley tobaccy what was agin' in the tobaccy barn. Ever'thing he owned was lost exceptin' for his debts. Phoebe paid 'em all off with the swap of the farm to Mr. Mac, exceptin' for them twelve acres what she saved for you. Them's the best acreage on the whole darn spread and you know it! She struck a sharp bargain. You should be proud of her and thankful.

"Not only that, she didn't keep nothin' for herself. Didn't need to, on account of some Yankee pharmacist she met while she was a volunteer nurse at the Red Cross. Name's DeLair Aubrey. He was in the Army too, a captain in the Medical Department. They got hitched and moved to his hometown - Jamestown, North Dakota, if'n you can imagine that. I ain't got a letter from her in awhile.

"Speakin' of letters, Phoebe sent you several in care of that

Army hospital you was stayin' at in Washington, D.C. She said she never heared from you. Didn't you get 'em?"

"Nope. Sorry. I'm drawing a complete blank."

"Well, you must've knowed something or you wouldn't 'ave come back here."

"Probably so. I just can't remember. Where's here besides Rabbit Hollow? What day is it? Heck, I can't even recollect what year it is."

"Here is Lawrence County, Kentucky. That's what. You was borned here! We're about forty miles south of Ashland. That ring a bell?"

"I rode a train which stopped in Ashland!"

"That's a start. Anything else?"

"Nope. What day is this?"

"It's Saturday. It's also the 3rd of April, 1920, in the Year of Our Lord. You been gone about three years. You and me is the same age. We're 24. My birthday's January 16th and yours is February 29th. Everyone always figured you was blessed - that you was special - on account of you bein' born on Leap Day. You're what they call a leapling.

"You and me growed up together. You're standin' on my pappy's farm. Now it's mine. I got 112 acres of prime hardwoods. You and me went to school together. We completed all eight grades at the Clifford School when we was sixteen. Miss Theobald was our teacher. I was sweet on Francine Wallace. You remember her, don't ya? Me and her got hitched when I was eighteen and she was sixteen. She died of the Spanish flu a year ago. The Lord never blessed us with no younguns. She's buried over yonder in the family cemetery.

"You wasn't really sweet on no one in particular. We all

thought maybe something would develop betwixt you and Jennifer Arnold but it never did. She married that Nettles boy, Gilchrist, right after we finished grade school. He's a dry goods clerk now. They live in Clifford and got two girls.

"After you and me graduated, I went to full-time farmin' right here on my pappy's spread. You up and went to high school in Louisa. You lived over your Uncle Malcolm's grocery with him and your Aunt Flo and all their kids. We thought they was gonna turn you into a grocer. You graduated in 1916 and moved back here, but we could all see you wasn't happy to be tied down on no farm.

"You lit out and got a job as a fireman on the L&N Railroad. Next thing we heared, you up and joined the Army and went off to war in Belgium or France or some darn place. Then we heared you was wounded and was recoverin' in a military hospital in Washington, D.C. Any of this comin' back to you?"

"Nope. I wish it did."

"Well, last I heared, Phoebe wrote you, but you never wrote back. I figured maybe you was dead or disfigured or you lost your mind or somethin'. Looks like I was right about my last guess.

"You said you was hungry. Let's get off our feet for a little bit. I'll make you some pork sausage and grits. Even got some fresh eggs and milk. The hens is laying good and the cow provides me more milk than I can drink. You'll have to go fetch a jug out of the spring house. Surely you remember where that is."

"It's starting to come back a little bit. Thanks. I don't recall the last time I ate. I can bake us some biscuits if you have the fixings."

"I do. It's a deal. My biscuits ain't nearly so good as Francine's was."

Chapter 2:
Formulating a Plan

Jack and Gerard spent the rest of the morning cooking and eating and getting reacquainted. Gerard said if Jack wasn't in a gol-dern hurry to get to wherever he was going to, he was welcome to stay as long as he pleased. It was nigh on time to plow and sow the fields and he could use the help but he ain't got no money to pay for labor. He said he aimed to plant a one-acre garden of vegetables for home consumption and thirty acres of corn for revenue.

Jack asked where he took his corn to market.

Gerard replied, "You certainly have lost your memory or you wouldn't need to ask.

"A small portion of the corn is for the livestock plus I eat some myself. I got two draft horses, Mabel and Jerome, and two saddle mules, Oscar and Tulip. I got one milch cow. Her name's Matilda. Then I butcher a pig each fall for meat but I don't name him on account of I aim to eat him. Don't think it would be fittin' to eat an animal I named."

"Your animals eat corn?"

"The pig does and in a manner of speakin' the others do too, especially the horses and mules if'n the corn is sweet."

"Hmm."

"Usually, I got around two dozen chickens and I feed them some corn but I eat the ones what ain't good layers so the numbers vary. Speakin' of chickens, the pooch and I have our work cut out for us keepin' the foxes out of the henhouse.

"I sell most of the eggs to Woodrow Falstaff a couple of times a week, which he sells out of his general store down at the crossroads at Clifford Pike and the Louisa Road. Remember his store? Plus, I sell him several dozen bushels of corn when it's in season so long as it's sweet. He'll also buy up whatever fresh milk I don't need, which is nearly all of it. Mostly, betwixt the eggs and the milk, he keeps me in coffee and sugar and smoking tobaccy and whatever else I need like ammo or oncet in awhile shoes or clothes. I grow a little tobaccy to make my own plugs for chewin' but it ain't that good for smokin'.

"Gettin' back to the corn, I sell a little bit just so's I can honestly say it's a cash crop but that ain't the real reason I grow it. I got me a three-barrel still out in the woods and that's how I make most of my income. I'm small potatoes as far as sellin' liquor is concerned but I make a good product and sell it at a fair price. I ain't greedy and I don't take no chances sellin' to strangers nor folks I don't know real well.

"I don't want no trouble with the big outfits. A man could get his self arrested or kilt if he got too big for his britches. I'm pretty sure Sheriff Harned knows I make a few quarts, but like I said, I keep my head down low plus my shine is top shelf. It's pure, smooth, and ain't got nothin' harmful in it like lead or dead possums or such as that in the mash. It breaks a good bead and it's always a hunnert proof and then some. It ain't gonna inflame your gullet nor your guts nor make you go blind."

"You mean Moses Harned, the state fair champion hog caller, is high sheriff?"

"Yep."

"Ain't he a Baptist?"

"Yep, but if it wasn't for the Baptists, I'd only have a one-barrel operation instead of a three-barrel rig. Shucks! I'm a member of the Holy Ghost Baptist Church myself but I don't advertise my product at the alter. Heck! Jesus turned water into wine. Says so in the Good Book! Why can't I turn corn into moonshine? Besides that, some of my best customers belongs to the church. One of 'em is a deacon but I ain't saying who."

"How much shine you make in a year?"

"Oh, it varies. I'd say maybe three hundred gallons for profit. It all depends. It's better to cook it during the cooler months but it takes the mash longer to ferment. It's hard work. I stock up in the winter so I'll have a steady supply in the spring when I get back to farmin'. I store it in gallon jugs but sell it in quart jars.

"It took me a long time to build up my inventory of gallon jugs. I got plenty now. I ask all my customers to return the empty jars. Some does and some doesn't. The reason is, I try to keep the mercantiles from getting too darn nosy. Besides Falstaff's, I get jars from the Sears and Roebuck catalogue and sugar from Ellicott's Mercantile in Louisa whenever I'm over that way. If'n I was to start buyin' Ball jars twenty or thirty cases at a time, it wouldn't be no time afore the law or some greedy evildoers would be on me like white on rice. A single man like me don't have no need to do that much cannin'. Understand?"

"I do. How much you sell it for?"

"A buck a quart. That may sound high to you but my profit is only half of that and it's a lot of hard work. Afore Prohibition, my shine was only two bits cheaper than run-of-the-mill, eighty-proof bourbon. Today, bootleg store-bought whiskey is three or four times that if'n you can even get it and then it's prob'ly rotgut.

"All I can say is, 'thank you' to all the fools who voted in the Volstead Act. They ought to have had more sense than to try to separate a man from his whiskey but they didn't.

"What they done, is to make outlaws out of everyone who makes or sells alcohol or even drinks it! They thought they was making folks who likes to imbibe illegitimate, but that's darn near everyone 'cause most folks likes to drink now and then. So, when there is more illegitimate folks than legitimate, the illegitimate become the legitimate and vice versa. Think about it. Are there more bastards than kids whose folks are married? Of course not! It's like the tail wagging the dog!"

"I follow your logic but I bet the teetotalers never thought about it that way."

"No doubt. Remember when you asked if my livestock eats corn and I said in a manner of speakin'?"

"Yep."

"Well, there's certain folks that I trade moonshine to for the things I need and don't grow myself. Example. I don't grow oats. Old Man Bailey and his four boys do. They also like shine. I trade them shine for oats which I feed to the horses and mules, especially in the winter. I figure the corn what goes into the shine I trade for oats is their share of the corn. What I trade for necessities is separate from what I consider shine sold for profit."

"Gerard, you don't have to justify your business to me. Volstead is why my flask is empty. Darn all the teetotalers! Besides, it's got to be hard for you to make do when you're all alone. Farming's an iffy proposition anytime, especially if you ain't got a wife or kids to help out. Two bad years would put almost every farmer into bankruptcy. This brings me to my point. Would you like some help?"

"The short answer is 'yes' but you need to think about it carefully. There's always a risk of bein' raided by the sheriff and gettin' the still all busted up and windin' up in jail if'n he gets pushed too hard by the Prohibitionists. However, he has to have twelve teetotalers on the jury to convict. That would never happen unless the jury was stacked by the judge or commonwealth attorney, but I know both of them likes to take a nip so this ain't nothin' too serious to worry about.

"Worser than the law though, is the possibility of gettin' robbed or kilt by thieves who don't want to go to all the trouble of making their own elixir or because they're in the business theirselves and want to rub out the competition. Truth is, I reckon this is even less likely than gettin' raided by the sheriff 'cause I'm a small fry in the liquor business. I ain't takin' no business away from none of them big city boys nor would I want to. The bottom line is, I don't believe either of these possibilities are worth losin' sleep over, but they's still a risk. If'n you make shine, accordin' to the law, you're an outlaw."

"I'm all in, but I still have a few more questions."

"Glad to hear it. Shoot."

"Where do you store your product?"

"They's a couple of caves on my property nobody but me knows about. Even you don't know about 'em from all them years roamin' around here as a kid. They're well hidden. Plus, I'm always careful whenever I go to either one."

"How about the still?"

"It's well hidden too, but it's easier to find than my stash. I got some telltales set up on the farm and if'n I catch someone sneakin' around, it'll be to their dismay. That's all I got to say about it. Up to now I ain't aware of no one who's curious enough or stupid enough to come lurkin' about but that could always change. It goes without sayin' that the two of us can do a better job runnin' the business and keepin' a weather eye out for trespassers than me all by myself."

"You bet. How often do you sell your product?"

"Normally twicet or thricet a week assumin' I have the stock. I have set locations I check periodically. Buyers leave the cash, usually in their empty jar, and check the next day for a resupply. I seldom do a hand-to-hand but I do oncet in awhile."

"All righty, then. I'm ready to begin today but first I need to buy some clothes and a gun. Does Woodrow Falstaff sell clothes and guns as well as groceries? If he does, I'll buy what I need today."

"Hopefully you'll remember Woodrow and his store when you see him. He sells 'bout ever'thing a body needs but you don't really have to go today unless'n you just want to. You and me are 'bout the same size. I got some old clothes you can have for free unless'n you just want some new duds. Also, I got a twelve-gauge, double-barrel shotgun that your pappy traded to me that you can have. I also got some buckshot to go with it. Consider that my gift to you for joinin' up."

Well, that's mighty kind of you. I accept, but I still need to buy some clothes and I may want to get me a revolver or a rifle. When do you normally go to town? Don't you need to trade some eggs or milk?"

"Well, this is Saturday. Normally I wouldn't go until Monday. I go to church tomorrow and you are welcome to come. In fact, I hope you do. I don't have no second set of church duds to give you but you can certainly wear what you got on. You're a bonafide war hero and a lot of folks would like to shake your hand and thank you for your service. However, the war's been over for a year-and-a-half and you might get some nosy questions as to why you're still in uniform. If'n you prefer not to satisfy their curiosity, we better go to the store and get you some duds today. We can hitch up the horses and go take care of business right now."

"Let's do it, but before we go, let me change into those work clothes you offered. I'll return 'em soon as I buy my own. Also, I'd like to take a gander at the shotgun to see if it satisfies all my needs. I don't mean to look a gift horse in the mouth, and as the sailors say, 'any port in the storm will do', but I'd rather be safe than sorry. Maybe I won't need to buy a gun after all."

"You bet."

Gerard went into the bedroom while Jack waited in the main room. (The bedroom was the only other room in the cabin.) When he returned, he had a pair of well-worn overalls and a long-sleeve white shirt in one hand and the shotgun in the other. He handed it all to Jack. Then he said, "By the way, you can keep them clothes. I got enough to suit my needs. Maybe that'll save you a couple of bucks."

Jack uttered a sincere thanks. He set the clothes down on a chair. He examined the shotgun carefully. It was a well-maintained Remington with twin full-choke bores and rabbit-ear hammers. The barrels were 28-inches long. There was some wear on the bluing but no rust. The butt stock had a checkered English grip (instead of a pistol grip). The butt and fore stocks had been treated with linseed oil and rubbed down with boiled chicken leg bones to preserve the wood. This gun was in great shape! It didn't look like it was more'n ten or fifteen years old. Why didn't he remember it?

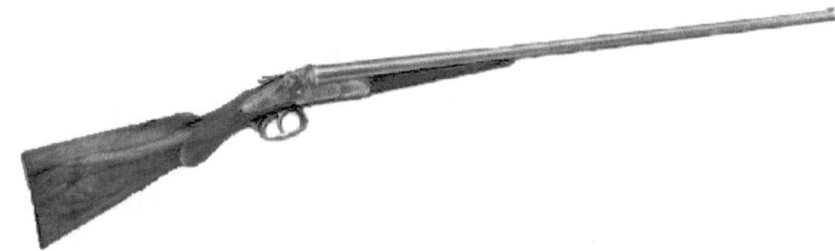

Jack broke it open. Two wax-treated cardboard shells were ejected about a half-inch from the breech (so you could grasp them with your fingers. Empty shells would eject five or six feet away.) He inspected them thoroughly. They were Peters brand, double-aught buckshot, meaning that each shell held nine .33 caliber balls. The full-choked 28-inch barrels would maintain a decent spread of the nine balls, but no more than thirty or so yards. Any shot farther than that aimed at a man's chest might only result in one hit - or none. Getting closer would certainly be better.

Jack would have preferred number four buck, which has 27 .23 caliber balls. The pattern of 27 balls would be much tighter than one with only nine, and thus should be effective (more hits) out to forty yards. It could well mean the difference between life and death.

Jack asked, "Where did my pappy get this gun? I don't recollect it."

Gerard responded, "Do you remember your Uncle Clive Jamison? I think your pappy said he lived up in Boyd County somewhere near Ashland. He was married to your momma's sister, Nellie. He was a blacksmith."

"I vaguely remember the name. I think I saw him once when I was a youngun. If he's the man I'm thinking of, he was fat and jolly. How do you know all this?"

"Your pappy told me. Anyway, the gun belonged to Clive. He died of apoplexy and Nellie asked your daddy to sell it. I needed a gun and he sold it to me. I give ten bucks for it. She th'owed in several boxes of shells and a cleanin' kit, too.

I told your pappy I was skinnin' him. He said no never mind. Nellie was some kind of Women's Christian Temperance Union battle axe who disliked alcohol, tobaccy, firearms, and men in general and truthfully all she wanted was to get rid of the darn thing. He said he would've kept it for hisself except'n each time he looked at it he was reminded of her and how much she made him want to throw her into a pit full of nasty, aggravated vipers. I give him the money and he give it to her and we three all felt like we come out ahead. Anyway, you was gone in the Army I s'pose, so that's why you don't remember this gun."

"Well, how about instead of you giving me this gun, I buy it for ten dollars? Then I can feel like I came out ahead, too?"

"You're twistin' my arm. I'll take it, but it's completely unnecessary. I feel like you should have it since it was in your family. It's all that's left for you but them twelve acres. If'n you really want to buy it, you can have the cleaning kit, too. I'll give you what's left of the buckshot but it's only about a dozen shells. I done shot all the number sixes what come with it."

Jack shelled out his single eagle and handed it to Gerard, who pocketed it and scurried back into his room. He returned with a half-box of Peters double-aught buck, the cleaning kit, leather carrying case, and a leather sling he got with the shotgun that he had removed because he didn't use slings.

Jack thanked him and asked, "Out of curiosity, what kind of guns do you own?"

"Well, I got me a Harrington and Richardson (most folks call it an H&R), single-shot, sixteen-gauge shotgun, which was my first gun. I still use it for small game and bird huntin'. I also got my new Winchester lever-action rifle. It's a .30-30 caliber. Holds eight rounds if'n there's one in the chamber. It's my go-to gun for deer and scoundrels.

"Oncet I took up the liquor business serious-like, I got me a .32 caliber Iver Johnson, Owl Head, five-shot, break-top revolver with a three-inch barrel. This'n is nickel-plated. Cost me five bucks, which is a lot cheaper than Colt or Smith and Western. I carry it in my pocket when I'm out and about and can't very well tote my rifle. And afore you ask, I got at least forty ca'tridges for each of 'em."

"Sounds like you're well-heeled if the Yankees up and decide to pick a war again."

"Darn tootin' I am. Get yourself changed while I hitch up the wagon with Mabel and Jerome."

Chapter 3:
Re-entry into the Public Domain

Thirty minutes later Gerard and Jack and the yellow pooch named Mosby were headed down the road in the farm wagon pulled by Mabel and Jerome en route to Falstaff's General Store, which was three miles away at the crossroads called Lonesome Corner.

Along the way Jack began to see landmarks that he remembered. Things like an ancient oak tree where legend had it that a highwayman was hanged for robbing and murdering a man and his family during the Revolutionary War because he thought they were carrying gold. Also, the derelict covered bridge spanning Buffalo Creek and the brick works which went out of business when he was a tyke. By the time they arrived at Lonesome Corner, he was beginning to feel like he was back at home. It was a welcome feeling.

There were two other wagons and one Tin Lizzy parked outside Falstaff's. A couple of farmers were sitting in rockers out front under the veranda sipping on ginger ales. One was smoking a cigar; the other a pipe. They both greeted Gerard warmly. They nodded politely at Jack and he nodded back.

There were three women and a man browsing around in the back of the store. Another man and woman were at the cash register. The man behind the counter had to be Woodrow Falstaff. He looked up at Gerard and Jack and said, "Good to see you all. Look around. I'll be with you whenever you all are ready."

Gerard replied, "You bet." Then he directed Jack to the shelving where the men's garments were stacked. He pointed to a counter along the back wall where the firearms, ammunition, and knives were located. He said, "I'll meet you at the gun counter after you pick out the duds you want."

It didn't take Jack long to make up his mind. It wasn't as if the selection were overwhelming. He bought two pairs of drawers, two undershirts, four pairs of socks, two red bandannas, a white, long-sleeve shirt, a pair of bib overalls, a brown fedora, a black tie, a pair of brown clodhoppers, a denim work jacket, and a pair of leather work gloves. He quickly estimated the cost of these items at twenty dollars, and decided that he needed to pass on buying a handgun until he earned a little money. Nevertheless, he wanted to see what type of firearms was readily available.

He carried his loot over to the gun counter and laid it down. Mr. Falstaff was already there jawing with Gerard. He said, "Jack, I thought that was you. It's been a long time. How the heck are ya?"

"Fine, Mr. Falstaff. Thanks for asking. I pray you and the family are doing well, too. You're right. Not by design, but it's been a real long time since I've been in this neck of the woods. I'm still getting reacquainted."

"Well, we're happy you come home. Gerard said you recently got discharged out of the Army. Thank you for your service.

"Are ya planning on sticking around, or do ya have something else in mind? By the way, me and the missus are broken up about what happened to your folks in that fire. It was just terrible. Please accept our condolences."

"Thank you, Sir. I'm still coming to grips with it. I didn't know. I just found out today. Cousin Gerard told me. Here's the thing. I didn't even mention this to Gerard yet. Didn't plan on telling anybody but I might as well put it out there so people won't look at me all funny-like.

"I joined the Army in April of '17 when the word went out they were looking for volunteers to fight the Germans. At the time, I was working for the L&N out of Louisa. The Army assigned me to the 17th Infantry Regiment in the 1st Division. They sent us to France. We saw a lot of action.

"In early November, 1918, I'm not certain of the day but it was during my unit's four-day rotation on the front line. (We did four days on and four days off.) The Jerrys started shelling our position with heavy artillery in preparation for an attack. One of their shells landed in the section of the trench where my squad was located. I never saw it. Don't remember hearing it. Never knew it happened.

"The next thing I remember is I woke up in an Army field hospital. My vision was blurred. I couldn't hear. My head was pounding. I was wrapped up like a mummy. I went in and out of delirium.

"After that, I woke up in a hospital ship. I vaguely recall being offloaded into an ambulance. They put me in the Army hospital in Washington, D.C. I didn't know who I was or how I got there. Heck, I didn't even know the war was over!

"Eventually, I learnt about the artillery barrage that wounded me. They said I was under a pile of bodies. They thought everyone was dead but when they uncovered me, they saw that I was still breathing. Everyone in my squad and many others from my platoon were kilt. Sixteen is what I heard.

"I have shrapnel wounds all over my body but they were the least of my injuries. I had a serious concussion. My vision was the first thing to clear up. Then my ears. I can't hear as good as before but I ain't deaf. I had amnesia. It took me nine months before I could function normally, and then I still didn't remember much.

"Last summer they put me to work at the hospital, one of the walking wounded, doing manual labor - mopping floors, burning trash, trimming bushes, that sort of thing. Come autumn, they gave me a clerical job. I filed reports, ran errands, guided visitors around the hospital who came to see loved ones, and so forth.

"Must of been about a week ago, they gave me an honorable discharge with credit for three years of service and a new uniform. They paid me what I had accrued and gave me a train ticket back to Louisa. That's it. I got no complaints. I would do it again if we had another war and they needed me.

"Cousin Gerard took me in and offered me a job on his farm, at least until I get back on my feet. I need a few things. That's why I'm here. Until now the only thing I owned was the uniform on my back and what few things that were stuffed into my ditty bag. Gerard said I own twelve acres from what's left of my grandpappy's farm. He fed me this morning. He gave me the clothes I've got on.

"The last thing I want is sympathy or folks looking at me like I'm a dimwit because I may not recognize them or know what they're talking about. More and more, the longer I'm here things are coming back to me. I'm telling you this so you can repeat it to anyone who asks and maybe save me from telling it again and again."

"My word! This is incredible! I can't thank you enough for your service. I applaud your grit and determination. How about you, Gerard?"

"Well, Jack told me straight off he had amnesia but he didn't tell me the rest. I'm tickled pink that he's decided to stay with me. We settled up today on a shotgun that was in his family that his pappy sold me. I think he needs some ammo or maybe wants to look at your revolvers. That's why I was waitin' for him over here."

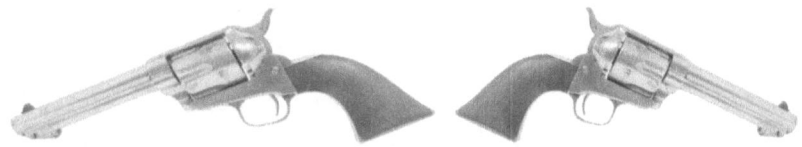

"Yes. Of course. What can I get you, Jack?"

"Do you have any twelve-gauge shells in number four buck?"

"I do. Your choice of Western or Peters brand. Same price. A buck twenty-five for a box of twenty-five."

"I'll take a box of the Peters. I also need some gun solvent, light machine oil, and some cloth rags for patches."

"Comin' right up. What else can I get you?"

"Well, I won't buy it today, but I'd like to look at that .38 caliber Smith & Wesson revolver over there."

Mr. Falstaff brought it out from under the counter. Jack looked at it with appreciation. It was beautiful. The bluing was deep and smooth. The grips were checkered walnut. It had a five-inch barrel. The balance was perfect. The cylinder held six rounds. He asked, "How much does this gun go for?"

"Normally $15 dollars, but for a veteran, I give a ten percent discount on all firearms. And just so you know, bullets are two-and-a-half bucks for a box of fifty. A nickel a shell if you buy 'em by the box. Otherwise eight cents per cartridge."

"Thank you, Sir. Hopefully I will be back one of these days before long and purchase it or another one like it. Oh, I also need a can of brown shoe polish and some tooth powder along with this pile of duds over here."

"You bet. Go ahead and take this to the counter and I'll ring you up."

Jack drove the wagon on the way back to Cousin Gerard's farm, otherwise known as Rabbit Bluff. Gerard said Jack needed to get familiar with the animals so they would behave for him when he was by himself. Along the way, Gerard said, "Here's the deal, Cousin. You help me do the farm work for no pay. We're equals on ever'thing. You can use the animals like they was your own. I got a couple of saddles in the barn if'n you want to ride instead of drive.

"I got an Army cot in the shed you can sleep on. You can set it up anywhere you like in the cabin where you can find the space. If'n you decide to stick around long enough we'll get a bed. Heck, I might be able to get one anyway cheap from Old Mrs. Thackeray. Her husband's dead and her kids is all grown up and she's probably got one she would sell for cheap. Might even swap her a couple of quarts for it since I heard she likes a little nip in the evenin'.

"I done told you my profit is fifty cents on each quart of shine I sell. I will pay you twenty cents for every quart we sell from here on out. Liquor used to barter with don't count. That shine is factored in as receivin' something for the common good. Part of my expenses. Not counted as profit. If'n we have a good year, you should make sixty bucks or so and you don't have no overhead. I'll make about ninety but all the overhead is mine. You good with that?"

"I am. I think that's more than generous. I am completely satisfied with these arrangements.

"What about this? You said you wanted to stay small so as not to put a target on your back. That's smart. I agree a hundred percent. However, you might want to consider this. Two of us working together can accomplish more than one man farming and making shine all by himself.

"For example, we might be able to produce four hundred quarts for sale without breaking into a sweat. Maybe stockpile more for summer consumption. Of course, that would be absolutely unnecessary unless you have a hard time filling the needs of your clientele now. I'm not suggesting that you incur more risk by taking on unknown buyers, just that you sell more shine to existing customers if there's a demand. You would still be operating at low risk.

"Also, another consideration is this. Prohibition is only a few months old. The demand for alcohol is bound to be higher now since so many traditional outlets are shut down. Do you know what your competitors are charging for a quart? I realize you produce a better product than them but what do they charge for an inferior product?

"Also, has the price of sugar gone up? If so, you might want to stockpile some before it goes up even higher. I guess what I'm really asking is this. What if you raised the price to a buck-ten? Would that be more or less than your competitors? Perhaps this is not the time to raise the price but if the price of sugar does go up, you may have to consider it."

"Dang, Cousin! You're a sly devil, ain't ya? I'm glad we're workin' together. I agree we should up production. I do have spells where I'm out of product. I prob'ly need to buy another hunnert jugs but I'll do it twenty at a time. Also, I'm not lookin' for new buyers. I get a few extra each year just by pickin' up relatives I know from the buyers I already have.

"I do need to stock up on sugar. Either you or I need to head over to Ellicott's Mercantile over in Louisa this week. You, I think. In case you forgot, that's about sixteen miles. That's a couple of long days back and forth. Tell Rafe Ellicott you're my cousin. He won't ask no questions. If'n I was you, I'd sleep at

Homer Spellman's Livery Stable for free but if'n you don't like that, you can stay at Miss Melinda's Boarding House just up the street. Also, you can pick up two dozen gallon jugs and two cases of jars. I'll get a jump on the plowin' while you're gone. I'll give you the money Monday morning afore you leave.

"Oh yeah, I suggest you bypass Lonesome Corner so ever'body doesn't know our business. Avoid unasked questions or curious looks. Cut off at the old brickyard and foller that road about two miles. It'll dead-end back at the Louisa Highway. Any questions?"

"Nope. You sure you don't want me to stay home and plow?"

"Not this time. I got milk and eggs to take to Falstaff's and a half-dozen drop sites to check. I ain't had time to learn you the ropes on all that yet, so you go to Ellicott's. Maybe I'll do it next time."

"Okay. How long you think it'll take us to plow and sow the fields?"

"Well, about five days to plow, maybe six, if'n we go sunup to sundown which we won't. I only have one plow but we can take turns and it should go a little faster. Less wear and tear on the horses, too. Maybe next year if'n you stick around I'll buy a second plow. It'll take us the better part of this month to get the fields plowed and sown with time in between to take a breather. Plus you never know what Mother Nature will throw at us. Could rain a week straight. You know how it is. You been through all this afore."

"I have and that's why I became a railroader. However, I never thought about nor had an opportunity to become a distiller. That really suits my fancy. Also, I understand the wisdom of 'stay small, stay long.' Smart. Live modestly and avoid attention. Therefore, I choose to earn my keep farming in order to learn distilling from a master. It beats running off to some big city to work for a bootlegger, which is really nothing more than signing on for wages to be a gun thug. Never learn the craft and probably wind up in an early grave. Not only that, we're working for ourselves, not someone else.

"Understand, L&N treated me very well. I got no complaints but after a tour in the Army I'm ready to live my life with a lot less structure. No more shaking hands with the clock. But if distilling weren't in the equation, I'd probably try to get my old job back even though being a fireman on a locomotive is backbreaking work. I was either freezing or burning up. Even so, I knew in time, I'd get a shot at being an engineer and that was my goal. Now my goal is to learn how to be a distiller."

"Fair enough. I'll learn ya right."

Chapter 4:
Step One in Learning the Business

On Monday morning, Gerard and Jack got up well before dawn since they had a full day's work ahead of them. Gerard collected the eggs and milked Matilda. Jack fed a bag of oats to the horses and mules, mucked the stalls, slopped the pig, and spread scratch out for the chickens. Once the animals were tended to, they fed themselves. By the time Jack commenced his journey, the sun was just breaking over the horizon.

It was a beautiful spring day. Jack was thrilled that buying supplies was his task instead of plowing fields. He knew how to farm and it wasn't something he particularly enjoyed. Even so, he knew all of life was a trade-off - that oftentimes you have to do something you don't like in order to do what you do like. He knew he would be behind the plow when he returned. That's just the way it is.

Once upon a time Jack had been familiar with the road to Louisa but it had been so long ago, it was almost like he was charting new territory. He took the bypass to avoid Lonesome Corner just like his cousin suggested. He didn't encounter any fellow travelers until after he returned to the Louisa Road. They waved greetings to each another but didn't stop to chat. Guess these strangers had a long trip ahead of them, too.

He arrived in Louisa mid-afternoon. He was ravenous. Lunch had consisted of a few sausage biscuits left over from breakfast. His first impulse was to stop by a cafe and eat but he held back. Best he meet Rafe Ellicott and tend to business. Then he would take care of himself.

Rafe had a busy concern going here. Jack saw three employees besides the owner. The store was doing a thriving business. When it was his turn at the counter, Jack introduced himself as Gerard's cousin. Rafe asked, "How's his wife doing? I heared she was ill."

Jack responded, "It must have been a long time since Gerard was here. She passed away last year. I thought he would have mentioned it."

"Right. Just checkin'. Never seen you afore. Some of my customers is sketchy. Don't like folks pryin' into their business. I feel the same way myself. You never know if the person you're talkin' to is a snitch for the federal revenue men or someone even worser.

"Things has gotten dicey since Volstead. More strangers around town than ever afore. Most of 'em come in threes and fours in big fancy automobiles. I seen a couple with Ohio license plates. You don't have to worry much if they's from West Virginny. No big cities there.

"Yep, it's a rotten shame when one of our own people fingers us to the sheriff or an outsider lookin' to skin us, and all because of a law none of us wanted in the first place."

"Dern tootin'. That's why Gerard sent me. I recently got discharged out of the Army. Most of my family perished and I lost all but a dozen acres of the family farm, the result of a lightning storm while I was overseas. I'm living with Cousin Gerard now. He's teaching me a new line of work. He couldn't come today on account of some other business he had to tend to. He prefers doing business with you to avoid prying eyes. He sent me to fetch three sacks of sugar, two dozen gallon jugs, four cases of Ball jars and and two boxes of Ball jar lids and seals."

"You know them sugar sacks is a hunnert pounds each, don't ya?"

"Yeah, he told me. He's stocking up in case the price goes up on account of demand."

"Well, it already has. Last time Gerard was here sugar was fifty cents a pound. It's gone up to 55. That's $165 just for the sugar. The jugs and the jars and lids will be another fifteen bucks. You got a wagon big enough to haul that much weight?"

"I do, but it'll be tight with the jars. I'll just have to be careful."

"Okay. That'll be $180."

"Jack gave me mostly one-dollar bills. Also he told me to ask if you could swap out another hundred bucks in paper currency for gold or silver."

"You're workin' for Gerard, all right. He don't trust paper money. Let's go back to my office and count it out and I'll see what I can do.

"Hayward, can you take over the counter for me?"

"Sure thing, Mr. Ellicott."

Once they were alone, Jack counted out $168 in ones, eight two-dollar bills, twelve five-dollar bills, and ten ten-dollar bills, for a total of $344. Subtracting $180 left $164. Rafe dropped down to the floor behind his desk and opened a hidden safe under a rug. He brought out a small metal lockbox full of coins. He handed Jack four double eagles, six single eagles, four half eagles, and four silver dollars. Rafe wrapped the paper currency with a rubber band, put it and the box back into the safe, and replaced the rug. Jack dropped the coins into a worn leather pouch with a drawstring and put it in the breast pocket of his bib overalls.

When they returned to the counter, Jack looked around to see if anyone was paying attention to him. It didn't appear so. Jack and Rafe shook hands. Then Rafe called for one of his employees, a brawny, dimwitted sixteen-year-old lad named Walter, to load the wagon. They covered the load with a canvas tarp and tied it down.

Jack drove his load over to Spellman's Livery Stable. Due to the value of the load, he agreed to let Jack park it inside the barn. Jack said he planned to sleep next to the wagon. Mr. Spellman charged Jack a buck to lodge and feed the horses and fifty cents to store the wagon inside.

Jack picked up his shotgun which was in the homemade leather sleeve Gerard had given him, and walked over to the Main Street Cafe next to the train station for an early supper. He devoured four pieces of fried chicken, a mountain of mashed potatoes with white gravy, green beans, biscuits, peach pie, and a carafe of cold, sweet tea. Boy! These women sure knew how to cook! Then he bought a half-dozen country ham biscuits wrapped in wax paper to eat for his breakfast and lunch tomorrow. He purchased some pipe tobacco and the Ashland newspaper at the general store on his way back to the stable. Might as well catch up on the news before it got too dark to read.

After dark, Jack rolled up into his blanket under the wagon, unsleeved shotgun next to his side. He enjoyed his best sleep in weeks.

The next morning as he was preparing to leave, Mr. Spellman took him aside and whispered, "Mr. Rabbit, you seem to be a nice young man. I know your cousin well. He always boards his animals with me when he comes to town.

"You need to tell him that we're startin' to see some elements here in Louisa all the way from Cincinnati. They wear fancy suits and drive expensive automobiles. They call theirselves businessmen who're just lookin' around for new opportunities.

"Fiddlesticks! What? Here in sleepy ol' Lawrence County? Do I look like I just fell off a turnip wagon? It's gotta be at least 150 miles from here to Cincinnati! They ain't got no business opportunities closer to their own town than Louisa? Hogwash! Ever' dang one of 'em is armed to the teeth. I even seen a tommy gun in one machine!

"I been told they're in the retail adult beverage business, like givin' alcohol a fancy name will make it all legal again. Also, they aim to corner the market, so help me God! I was informed by someone who knows ever'thing what goes on in this town that they was buyin' up all the liquor being made in these here parts for seventy-five cents a quart and then sellin' it for twicet that. Any moonshiner who don't get on board and sell all their hootch to them will be burnt out or kilt. Some folks think they ain't got no choice has done knuckled under. Two families went outta business and skedaddled. Just up and left in the middle of the night! That's how scairt folks are!

"Plus, our sheriff ain't no account. If'n he was, he'd a run these so-called, visitin' businessmen plumb outta the county but he didn't. Nosiree! He knows sure as shootin' these dandies ain't up to no good. Heck, he's got ears ever'where. He knows who makes liquor just like he knows who can hardly come up with his property taxes each year. Now it's true he ain't raided no stills yet, but he also ain't chucked the first one of them gun thugs in jail for threatenin' and kickin' the snot out of honest, hard-workin' folks.

"You think he ain't heared about that? Horsefeathers! They's less than 17,000 mortal souls in the whole dern county which also includes chil'ren. Many of 'em live right here in the county seat. Sheriff Harned's lived here his whole life! He knows ever'one. Folks voted for him 'cause they trusted him. He ain't blind! I suspect he's in cahoots with 'em. Either that or he's afraid of 'em. Mebbe they threatened him too! Wouldn't that be a fine kettle of fish?

"I know you're a good ways south of here but sooner or later these Yankee mobsters will find their way to your doorstep. I can almost guarantee that someone who was at Rafe's business yestiddy done seen what you was buyin' and found out who you was and where you're from. Not Rafe mind you, he's rock solid, but one of them slackers who's always hangin' around over there. Rattin' people out is how deadbeats who ain't never worked a day in their miserable lives make a livin' without workin' up a sweat.

"You better have your eyes wide open on your way back. If'n they confront you, you'll be outnumbered and outgunned. Maybe even surrounded. God bless, my boy. Tell Gerard 'Hey' for me."

"I will, Mr. Spellman. Thank you. Now I know what we may be up against."

The return trip took longer. He got a later start. The load was heavier and the horses had to work harder. Jack's head was on a swivel on alert for an ambush. His shotgun rested across his lap under his blanket. He had extra shells in the pockets of his bibs.

Daggummit! He didn't survive the war just to lay down and play scaredy-cat to some gangsters out of Cincinnati.

The trip was uneventful. It was almost dusk before he got back. Gerard was sitting on the verandah smoking a pipe and drinking some of his own elixir out of a white-speckled, blue enamel cup. A corked, brown, ceramic gallon jug was resting at his feet.

"Hey, Cousin. I was beginnin' to think ya got lost. Ever'thing work out okay?"

"It did. Let me take care of the horses and I'll fill you in."

"Carry on, Sir. You can leave ever'thing in the wagon. We'll move it tomorrow. I got some pintos simmerin' on the stove. We can sup whenever you're hungry. I'll fetch you a cup so you can have a wee taste with me afore we feed."

It took Jack a half-hour to tend to the horses. He checked the canvas tarp which covered the supplies. It was snug. It didn't look like rain but you can never tell this time of year. He picked up his valise, shotgun, and blanket, and headed to the verandah.

Gerard had already brought out another cane-bottom, ladder-back chair for Jack to sit on. He handed Jack a full cup of elixir. He sat down and took a sip. Smooth. He would have preferred bourbon aged in an oak barrel but this was the next best thing and likely would be for years to come. Better to acquire a taste for it now.

Jack reached into the chest pocket of his bibs and retrieved the leather pouch. He handed it to Gerard. Jack said, "That pouch has $162.50 in gold and silver coins. You gave me $344 in paper.

Sugar has gone up to 55 cents a pound. Three sacks was $165. The jugs, jars, and lids cost $15. Livery charges was $1.50. This is the balance."

"Didn't you eat? You was supposed to take that out of this, too."

"I did. Cost me about two bucks. I didn't figure that was on you."

Gerard poured the contents of the pouch into the palm of his hand. He returned the pouch to Jack. He separated both silver dollars and the half dollar and handed them to Jack also. He said, "Jack, I know you ain't flush right now. Anything you spend for food or lodging or anything else while you're on business is a bonafide cost of doin' business. It ain't no different than when I trade shine for oats, a saddle, or anything else we need to live. Buyin' stuff ya hafta have ain't counted in the profit. Got it?"

"Got it. Appreciate this. Truth is, I am a wee bit lean right now. I need to earn some money but I can make do until my labor helps generate sales.

"By the way, local current events ain't good at all right now. I got some bad news. Both Rafe and Mr. Spellman clued me in. They both also said to tell you 'Hey.'

"What did they tell you?"

"Big city gangsters most likely from Cincinnati, have swarmed into the area like locusts prior to the Exodus at least as far south as Louisa. They're flexing muscle, making no bones about it that they're taking over all the liquor business in Lawrence County. Word is they've already squeezed some of the local distillers, forcing them to sell every drop they make to them for 75 cents a quart which they turn around and retail for a buck-fifty. I guess most of the product is headed up north but they didn't say.

"They're well-armed and they got locals on the payroll snitching for 'em. Mr. Spellman claims they've been successful taking over some of the liquor business in the north end of Lawrence County. Maybe other counties, too. Not sure about that but it stands to reason that the longer the supply line the less the profit. Of course, weak sisters will always be knocked off first. Also, the counties where the law is bought off.

"Mr. Spellman thinks Sheriff Harned could be in cahoots with 'em. Either that or they've scared him up under the couch. He did say the sheriff hasn't busted any stills, but he also hasn't arrested any of these mobsters for threatening or beating up distillers who won't play ball. However, it's also possible that no one's come forward with a complaint. Apparently, no one has been kilt or burnt out yet. I'm sure we would've already heard if they had.

"He seemed certain that a number of locals have already knuckled under. Others decided to get out of the business. Supposedly two families up and moved to parts unknown in the middle of the night without telling a soul. He expects the hoodlums will eventually come farther south and put the arm on us and everyone else in our neck of the woods.

"He says they're all heeled. He saw a machine gun in one automobile. They usually travel three or four to a machine, sometimes two or three vehicles all together. Folks are scared. Easy to understand why when the hyenas travel in packs.

"He said it's likely somebody who was hanging around Rafe's fingered me as a moonshiner. He warned me to be careful on the trip back and I was. I didn't see anyone. He wanted me to warn you."

"Did he say who was beat up or kowtowed or quit or moved

away?"

"Nope. I didn't ask."

"What a sorry bunch of jackals! Not sure what to make of Sheriff Harned. We got a lot to do to get ready for hard times. We don't wanna get caught with our pants down.

"Let's eat. We got a full day tomorrow."

Chapter 5:
Working Like a Rented Mule

The next couple of weeks was backbreaking work plowing and sowing the fields.

This had to take precedence if they were going to eat and have corn to conduct their distilling operation. Jack did most of the farm work to free up Gerard to tend to the routine sales of elixir, and milk and eggs, not to mention other critical responsibilities, such as storing the sugar in the secret hideaway, the procurement of additional necessities, checking on existing telltales and setting up some new ones.

They both felt like they were racing against time in preparation for the day the hoodlums would show up and try to put the arm on them. Jack and Gerard both knew they wouldn't survive if they got caught off guard. They fully expected to be outnumbered, facing men who got paid to inflict pain, if not death. Both Gerard and Jack worked like rented mules to get ready. Their days were long and their nights were short.

Sunday was the Lord's Day - the only day they didn't work - but it also served another purpose besides rest and worship. After church they had an opportunity to catch up on local news beyond that which Gerard gleaned at Lonesome Corner on his egg and milk run. Some would call this gossiping. Others would call it intelligence gathering. Depends upon whose ox is being gored.

Their methodology was to divide and conquer. Jack ran interference and subterfuge, engaging the teetotalers, many of whom were the wives of the crowd Gerard was trading information with, otherwise identified as the closet moonshiners and imbibers. Discretion was the hallmark of those who wished to avoid a visit from the sheriff, or evildoers, or the preacher, who was working fervently to save souls, conventional Baptist wisdom being that the demon alcohol put one on the Road to Perdition without fail.

Jack didn't feel like a hypocrite. He sincerely believed that the Baptist faithful were doctrinally misinformed as it related to alcohol. This was a situation in which the Catholics and some of the other Protestant denominations were far more enlightened. What was the old adage? "Everything in moderation." That being said, if one wanted to share in Christian fellowship in this locale, the only option was deciding which Baptist church to attend. Besides, like Gerard said, they weren't advertising their wares at the alter.

So far, they had been fortunate. The hillbilly grapevine had no information regarding any distiller in close proximity who had been approached by the Yankees as they were euphemistically referred to. However, two large, black automobiles, a Packard and a Maxwell traveling together with six swells, were spotted filling their machines with gasoline at Maynard's Ashland Oil and Garage, located on the Ashland-Paintsville Highway in Ulysses.

Old Man Dempsey was there getting a couple of inner tubes patched for the tires on his Model T Ford. (Some careless fool spilt a box of nails on the highway!) The arrogant city slickers swooshed in stirring up a cloud of dust and grit with absolutely no regard to the customers who were outside waiting for service, smoking, chewing tobacco, drinking Coca Colas, and/or otherwise jawboning with each other. In fact, the inconsiderate interlopers burst out laughing when they saw the entire gaggle brushing the dirt off their clothes.

The unwelcome, pompous jackanapes piled out of their machines and strutted around in their posh suits like they were motion picture stars. They were flippant to Boyd Maynard when he told them the only toilet he had was the outhouse out back. What? No flush commodes out here in the sticks with the hicks?

Old Man Dempsey could see that at least three of the swells were wearing guns in shoulder holsters. They all looked like they would just as soon shoot you as get a shave and a haircut. Other customers made similar observations.

The brash strangers wanted to know where the Bostick farm was; said they heard it was for sale. Everyone there knew where Lige Bostick's farm was and that it wasn't up for sale, but they all pretended otherwise. Finally, Adrian Pullman spit out a stream of loose leaf tobacco juice on the right rear tire of the Maxwell. He said he wasn't for sure but thought it was along the dirt road going towards Inez maybe six or eight miles. He said they'd recognize it when they saw a barn with about twenty sets of deer horns nailed up over the door. Also because of the smell since Mr. Bostick was a pig farmer. Adrian said the road wasn't that good and that they might want to wait a day or two for the sun to dry up the mud.

Of course the wise guys didn't listen. They just piled into their machines and blasted off like they was late for dinner. They probably didn't make three miles before they bogged down and had to walk back for help to get winched out.

After they were gone, Adrian mounted his mule and plodded towards home in the opposite direction, most likely to warn Lige, who was his neighbor. Everyone got a big laugh at the expense of these uppity Yankees. All the locals knew the Inez road was a muddy quagmire and that the bridge was out over Adler Creek. Then they got to ruminating about it, and with hardly a word spoken, everyone scurried off in case the Yankees didn't get stuck too bad and decided to come back for some revenge.

The main thing all the witnesses took away from this event is that Lige Bostick and his boys have a four-barrel still and six mobsters were looking for him to make him an offer he couldn't refuse - or so the Yankees thought. Odds were, the Yankees would leave more of their own blood on the ground than they would take from Lige and his sons. Still, the hillbilly grapevine alerted everyone in Lawrence County who 'had a dog in the fight' and even some who didn't. By the end of the week, every general store for miles around had noticed a significant uptick in the sales of ammunition, guns, and dynamite. Some stores even ran out and had to special order more.

Gerard and Jack took heed. Now that the crops were planted,

they had time to tighten up their security and distill some more shine. Gerard and Jack rode the mules over every square inch of Rabbit Bluff, helping Jack get reacquainted. Jack had been over most of it when he and Gerard were younguns but he hadn't seen all of it, and anyway he didn't recall half of what he had seen back then.

Rabbit Bluff consisted of 112 acres, of which approximately seventy were primarily forested with hardwood trees. This was the hill acreage including some deep ravines, none of which were utilized in farming. It was left mostly undisturbed for the tranquility of unmolested land and for the wildlife, meaning whitetail deer, nocturnal bobcats, turkeys, squirrels, foxes, raccoons, opossums, wood ducks, hawks, owls, and so forth, including undesirable critters like black bears, skunks, porcupines, coyotes, woodchucks, timber rattlers, and copperheads. Definitely, too dang many copperheads.

The rest of the acreage made up the curtilage around the house, barn, and other outbuildings, the fenced pasture, the thirty-acre cornfield, and the one-acre vegetable garden. The same clearwater, limestone creek which ran through Jack's twelve acres, Rabbit Hollow, meandered through Rabbit Bluff. The water was so pure that Gerard's pappy, Elvis, didn't even dig a well for human consumption until 1905. He only dug it then to forestall complaints from his wife and older kids about constantly having to fetch water in buckets whenever they wanted a drink or to take a bath or wash clothes.

After checking seven different telltales which were undisturbed, Gerard took Jack to the still. It was situated next to a bluff deep in the woods. A branch of the creek ran right up next to it. This made for easy access to the water necessary to make the mash. Initially, Gerard had used wooden buckets to fill the barrels, but now he had a hand pump with a black rubber hose running from the branch to the still. This was a major labor-saving device. The woods also provided the fuel to heat the still. There was plenty of deadfall so he seldom had to cut down a healthy tree. When he did, it was nowhere near the still.

The entrance to one of the two caves on the property, the smaller one, was about eighty yards from the still. It was well-concealed. This is where Gerard stored the corn, sugar, and yeast to make the mash, empty gallon jugs to hold the finished, blended product, the coil and condenser when they weren't in use, various tools, and other necessary items needed to operate a still, plus a galvanized tub to blend the four-to-five runs from the same batch of mash to even out the finished product to a hundred proof.

The other cave was two hundred yards farther away and even harder to locate. Conceivably, it was just another entrance to the same cave. Nobody knew for certain. This is where Gerard stored the finished product in gallon jugs which he poured into quart Mason jars as needed for retail. In essence, this was his savings account.

The operation worked something like this, with the caveat that each distiller, moonshiner or otherwise, has his own recipes and modus operandi so variations are the norm.

For moonshiners it all begins with oak barrels which have a volume of 42 gallons. They fill the barrel(s) with the raw ingredients to initiate the fermentation process. Alcohol is derived from fermenting starchy vegetables, grain, or fruit. The moonshiner uses a mixture of corn, sugar, water, and yeast. This mixture is called mash. A standard ratio is a gallon of water to a pound of corn, a pound of sugar, and a small amount of yeast.

Legal distilleries don't add sugar to their mash because it isn't necessary. Mash (legal distilleries call it beer) will ferment without sugar but it takes more time. Also, instead of barrels they use huge wooden vats housed in warehouses which stay warmer year around than an outdoor, clandestine operation in the woods.

In a legal operation, the time-consuming part of making bourbon is in the aging process, not the fermentation or distilling process. The distillate is stored in charred oak barrels, usually for five or more years to create the sought-after smell and flavor. No small-time operator (moonshiner) could survive with this business model waiting that long to turn a profit, so they generally dispense with the concept of aging. That being said, it doesn't mean the moonshine is necessarily rough or coarse. It just means that the flavor is different. Think vodka, rum, or tequila.

Different flavors, but they all take the consumer to the same destination.

Moonshiners usually work in the woods and for good reason. It would be the height of folly to make liquor in your barn or outbuilding.

First, it might be detected by neighbors or visitors due to the smell of fermenting mash, who might feel compelled to alert the law.

Second, the law would be justified in arresting, prosecuting, and incarcerating the violator(s), demolishing the still (to include pouring out all the mash and alcohol), and seizing the building for lost tax revenue. (Moonshine is untax-paid alcohol since it's illegal to make it in the first place.)

Third, the violator's house or any other outbuilding is also subject to seizure if the finished product is stored in it. This disaster, which can be avoided by making moonshine in the woods, could be referred to as a trifecta for the law but it would be a triple whammy for a moonshiner who was this foolish.

The veteran moonshiner knows when the mash is ready to cook by its tackiness. He dips his hand into the fermenting mash and pulls it out. If his fingers are sticky, but not quite so sticky that they're difficult to separate, the mash is sufficiently fermented and ready to cook. It doesn't take an apprentice distiller very long to learn by doing just how tacky is the right amount.

Once the mash is ready, it's poured into the still which is heated over a wood fire. Since the cooker is sealed, the steam from the mash vaporizes and rises into a copper coil roughly six to eight feet long. The steam cools in the coil, turning into droplets of clear alcohol which are captured in another container.

On average, a barrel of mash will yield ten percent of moonshine per cooking. Also, each batch of mash can be cooked four or even five times to glean most of the alcohol it is capable of producing. However, each cooking results in a lower proof of alcohol. The first batch might be as high as 180 proof, sometimes referred to as grain alcohol. (Pure alcohol is 200 proof.) From there the proof diminishes each cooking to maybe 160, 100, 60, and down to perhaps 40.

Normally the batches of moonshine derived from each cooking (of the same mash) are blended together to obtain a consistent proof for each quart. In the example above, the result would be 108 proof alcohol in approximately a dozen or so gallons of moonshine (derived from five cookings of the same forty gallons of mash, the volume of which diminishes with each distillation.) The mash that's left over is good feed and makes for happy mules and horses and pigs due to the residual alcohol content.

Gerard's goal, besides producing a clean, pure, tasty, potent elixir, was not to sell any moonshine less than 100 proof. He despised distillers who watered down their shine for more profit and oftentimes to disguise an inferior, rougher product. Even so, he didn't have a fancy hydrometer like a legal distillery uses to proof its whiskey. Instead, he used the age-old method of vigorously shaking a sealed, nearly full jar of moonshine and watching the bubbles rise to the surface and dissipate. This is called checking the bead. The smaller the bubbles and the more quickly they disappear is a reliable indicator to distinguish between a good product and a poor one, as well as a way to determine the approximate proof. Of course, if the goal is to ensure the product is at least 100 proof, all one needs to do is pour a small amount into a fireproof container and strike a match to it. If it burns, it's at least 100 proof. If it doesn't, it's not.

Another concern with respect to the cooker and the coil is this. A prudent distiller avoids soldering joints to prevent lead from leaching into the liquor, which over time can cause blindness and death. Assuming the joints fit together tightly, the joints can be sealed with a flour and water dough mix which is allowed to harden. It won't last indefinitely, and in fact will have to be redone periodically, but it will certainly prevent heartbreak down the line.

Thus, endeth Jack's schooling in the art of moonshining. Concept explained to the apprentice, cogitated upon, and fully discerned, it was now time for OJT (on-the-job training). Jack and Gerard filled the barrels with the requisite ingredients to make the mash and covered them with lids held down with heavy stones (to keep the raccoons out) so the fermentation process could begin. One of them would check on it daily until it was time to begin distilling.

The sense of urgency to stockpile as much of a reserve as possible before the impending war between the forces of good and evil was not lost on either one of them. They both knew it was brewing and that they needed to be ready. They also knew they would have to fight their own battles against superior forces.

So, what else was new? This had been ingrained into their culture from the time their ancestors fled religious persecution by despotic kings in Great Britain during the seventeenth and eighteen centuries in pursuit of liberty. One way or another, their ancestors and they had been fighting for the continuation of these God-given rights since the day they were born.

Tyranny isn't the sole province of kings. Many lesser mortals have followed suit. Nevertheless, the fight against it is the same no matter the title of the oppressor. It ultimately results in one of two conditions - submission or resistance. Either can result in death.

The ultimate question is this. Do you want to die on your knees in submission to tyranny, or with a sword in your hand in defiance of same for everything you hold near and dear - life, liberty, property, and the pursuit of happiness?

Jack and Gerard had soberly pondered over this crucible long ago and each had come to an irrevocable decision. It was the same as the state motto in New Hampshire - 'Live free or die.' Most of the hill people in these parts felt the same way.

Chapter 6:
Learning the
Business Aspect of Moonshining

The next morning after chores, they saddled up the mules. Gerard preferred Oscar so Jack normally rode Tulip. They also put a pannier on Mabel to hold the moonshine they were going to deliver. Yesterday the same pannier was used on Jerome to haul corn. Of course Cousin Gerard and Jack were armed. They approached the big cave from a different direction than the day before to minimize blazing a highway directly to it that even a city slicker could follow.

They emptied four gallons of their stash into sixteen jars which they placed in the panniers. Jack counted 83 gallons of inventory when they were done. Gerard said that would last about two-and-a-half months.

They took a trail that went west from the backside of the property. It skirted Mr. Mac's property. At an old oak which had been struck by lightning, they went deeper into the woods about twenty yards to a boulder which was all by itself like it had fallen from the sky. It didn't really belong with the rest of the terrain. Next to the boulder were two empty quart jars. One of them contained a folded two-dollar bill. Gerard swapped two full jars for the empties. He said, "This is where I trade with Mr. Mac."

From there they rode another half-mile to a hollow tree in a copse of birch trees. This time it was a one-for-one exchange except the medium of exchange was Gerard's favorite - a silver dollar. "This is Widow Slocum's spot. For gosh sakes, don't never let on that you know she imbibes! She'll stop doin' business with me if'n you do. Her vice is a closely held national secret."

They continued on throughout the morning in this fashion, swapping out eleven jars. Several sites they checked were empty. Jack memorized the sites and who they were associated with.

The last stop on the route was Old Man Bailey's ramshackle farm. Gerard swapped three quarts of elixir for a hundred pounds of oats. While they were visiting, Mr. Bailey casually inquired, "Gerard, you had any unwelcome visitors at your place?"

"Nope. Someone lookin' for me?"

"Can't say for sure. My woman said Mrs. Campbell said that her old man told her that some city slickers stopped by Lonesome Corner and asked if'n he knowed how to get to your farm. They also asked directions to Clyde Higgins' place. Ain't you and him in the same side business?"

"You could say so, I s'pose. It's kinda like comparin' beefsteak to pork sausage. Clyde sells a second-fiddle grade of elixir in my estimation, but I confess. He does sell considerably more product than me. I heared he's got a five-barrel outfit. Did the strangers ask Mr. Campbell whilst they was in Mr. Falstaff's Store?"

"Nope. He was walkin' down the road after he done bought hisself a couple of plugs of chewin' tobaccy. They was in a big black machine. Four city slickers."

"What day did this happen?"

"Yestiddy."

"What did he tell 'em?"

"He said you lived about three or four miles down the road but you was a disagreeable cuss and stayed to yourself. Said you didn't like being around folks, especially strangers.

"He also told 'em where Clyde lives, except'n Clyde would talk a fence post to death and if'n they stop by his place they better plan on spendin' the whole dern afternoon. Said his old woman was even worser than him. Also warned that Clyde has a whole passel of geese runnin' loose in his yard and that they bite like the dickens."

"Thanks for fillin' me in. Haven't seen anyone around the old homestead yet but I reckon I ought to keep an eye out. We both know these Yankees don't have any business with Clyde or me that would be satisfactory to either one of us."

"You got that right. Good luck."

On the way back to Rabbit Bluff, Gerard and Jack discussed the new development. They decided that Jack would move his cot out to the barn just in case they had some midnight visitors. They also decided that they would have to check the woods a couple of times a day now just to make sure nobody found the still.

They were nearly home. They started to make the curve towards the front gate when they noticed fresh automobile tire tracks in the dirt. They pulled up short and cut back through the woods before they could be seen from the house. They tied Mabel and the mules next to a thicket out of sight from the road.

Gerard chambered a round in his rifle and placed the hammer on half-cock. He patted the right pocket of his farmers' jacket, double-checking that his revolver was still there.

Jack didn't need to check anything. His shotgun was always loaded. All he had to do was cock the rabbit ears and pull the triggers to unleash a horde of screaming lead balls to obliterate any threat within thirty yards. Not only that, his jacket pockets were always half-full with eight or ten shells of buckshot so he could continue to rain pee on his adversaries until they were no longer breathing or, God forbid, they snuffed the life out of him. For Jack, it was an all or nothing proposition. It was the same with Gerard.

They crept through the woods soundlessly like deer on a frosty morn. When they got near the edge of the tree line, they dropped down on their bellies and crawled even closer until they could see the front and the near side of the cabin.

A black Packard was parked up near the verandah. No doubt these were the passersby Mr. Campbell spoke to yesterday.

They watched for several minutes. Eventually they counted four men. All were wearing suits. Fancy clothes for a weekday out in the country. Two were wearing boaters. Two had on fedoras. They was even wearin' spats! Definitely city slickers.

Two men were sitting in the shade under the verandah in the ladder-back chairs on either side of the front door. Both were smoking. One was older and heavyset. He was smoking a long black cigar. He was probably the boss. The other was stubbing out a cigarette against the wall. Then he flicked the butt out in the yard where the chickens would probably eat it and get sick. No respect.

There were two others. One was sitting on the front steps. He was having a chew of loose-leaf tobacco and streaming gobs of spit at any chicken who wandered too close. The fourth man was coming out of the outhouse, pulling up his trousers. They could see he had a holstered gun on his belt. That meant the others were probably armed too, which is exactly what they expected.

Finally, they had taken in all that they could see. Gerard whispered, "Let's get back to the animals. You get on Tulip and cut through the woods. Circle around the back of the house. Try not to get spotted. Jack, you're my ace in the hole. Tie Tulip up someplace safe afore you get too close. We don't want her to get a whiff of them skunks and start hee-hawing.

"Cock both barrels when you get within shootin' distance. Try to do it afore they get a glimpse of you. If'n they see you cockin', they'll figure you're fixin' to shoot and go for their hardware, but if'n you've done cocked afore they see you, they'll figure out that slappin' leather would be their last stupid act on Mother Earth afore they're shakin' hands with the devil. What I'm hopin' for, is that they won't see you until it's too late to break bad. Are we clear?"

"Yep. What are you fixin' to do?"

"Me? I'm leavin' Mabel here. No need to give 'em even the slightest chance to find out I'm packin' two quarts of shine. No doubt they've already searched the house and the barn and ever'thing else. There ain't nothin' there to confirm their suspicions but we both know these fellers ain't goin' to give up that easily. They gotta be learnt a lesson. Just wish we didn't have to deal with 'em four at a time. This is when I wisht we had us a tommy gun.

"I aim to ride up a few feet from their machine and dismount. Hopefully, I'll be able to use the automobile for cover if'n we commence to shootin'. I can't predict how this will play out, 'exceptin' to say that I'll run 'em off my property and warn 'em to never come back.

"If'n they feel froggy and think four against one is sufficient to buffalo me they'll be sadly mistaken. Of course, I 'spect you to waste at least two of 'em afore they can do likewise to me. I'll take down one for sure but I might not have time to re-chamber another round or grab my revolver afore the last one gets me so be quick about reloadin' or I'll probably be a goner."

"Don't worry. If any two are close enough together, I'll get both with one shot."

"Okay. I'll wait about ten minutes afore I set out. That should give you enough time to get in position."

"Not to worry. I got this."

Jack had no trouble working himself behind the house without being seen. He tied Tulip to a sapling at the edge of the woods. He cocked both barrels of the Remington and surreptitiously walked from the back of the curtilage to the far side of the house opposite from where Gerard and he had been watching. Another eight feet and he would be in the front yard. He stayed where he was because he didn't want to cast a shadow that would extend to the front yard and give him away.

He listened for one of the gangsters to alert the others to the presence of Gerard. He didn't have to wait long. He heard, "There he is! Will ya look at that? Another hayseed riding a mule." They guffawed at their condescending joke.

A couple of minutes later, he heard the slow clip clop of hoof steps. One of the chairs scraped. Someone got up. Jack wanted to look but it was too early to step out. He needed to be sure all four sets of Yankee eyeballs were riveted on Gerard so he could step out undetected.

"About time you come home, Mr. Twyman. We have some business with you."

"I don't know any of you fellers. I ain't got no business with nary a one of you. Just pile in your machine and get off my property and don't never come back. This is the only warnin' you'll get. Next time I'll shoot first and ask questions later."

"Hey, Boss. This hick is full of hisself. Want me to learn him some manners?"

"Hold your horses! I haven't spoken my piece yet."

Jack eased around the corner. None of the city slickers noticed because they were zeroed in on Gerard, who had dismounted and was partially obscured by the automobile. He was holding his half-cocked rifle in both hands but the barrel was pointed towards the ground. He was flanked to his front about fifteen feet away on the left and the right by a thug on each side. Both had flat noses. One had a cauliflower ear. Both were obviously former boxers who had seen better days. Their proximity posed Gerard's greatest threat. The third palooka was standing about twenty-five feet away in front of the machine closer to Jack. His right hand was obscured because it was inside his jacket, probably resting on the butt of his gun. Oscar had turned away out of the line of fire and had started grazing in the grass. These pugs didn't worry him in the slightest.

The portly man rose up from the chair about twenty feet away and stretched. His lackadaisical and unconcerned demeanor expressed, "I'm important and in charge!" He commanded the other men to stand down. He spoke softly and calmly. In his best soothing, syrupy voice, he spoke, "Mr. Twyman, my name is Elgin LaRue. I'm a businessman from Cincinnati, Ohio. I represent a consortium that's expanding south into Kentucky.

"We're aware that you have a small side business as do more than a few of your fellow citizens in Lawrence County. We want to buy your product. All of it in fact, whatever you can produce on a continuing basis. We'll pay you a very fair price - 75 cents a quart.

"Many of your competitors have already joined our cooperative venture. We will be the sole retailer in Lawrence County, just as we are in several counties to the north of here like Boyd, Carter, and Elliott, just to name a few. We won't tolerate any independent operators.

"I'll give you a moment to mull over this one-time, very generous offer. You and I can shake on it and then we'll mosey along our way to the next stop. We'll come back tomorrow for the first delivery. We expect this to be a long, fruitful relationship for everyone concerned."

Gerard hissed back with barely contained rage. "Mr. LaRue, you can't shake me down like I'm some weak sister. My family fought Yankees like you and these here thugs more'n fifty year ago and we'll do it again if'n that's what it takes.

"This is your very last warning. Get back in your machine and don't never come back! Now I'll give you a minute to mull it over afore I start ventilating the whole lot of you, beginnin' with you first, Mr. LaRue. This moron closest to me will be next. Now get!"

Gerard raised his rifle, simultaneously pulling the hammer back to full cock and pointed it at Mr. LaRue's midsection. At twenty feet he couldn't miss. A .30-30 round fired from that range would be devastating to it's fleshy target. Of course, the three gunmen drew their hardware and aimed at Gerard so it wasn't looking good for him either, unless Mr. LaRue was absolutely convinced that Gerard would kill him before he died himself in a fusillade of bullets.

Gerard wasn't bluffing but even a slight miscalculation by Mr. LaRue would be fatal for both of them.

There was a pregnant pause, kind of a Mexican stand-off, which allowed Jack to say his piece. He said, "I got the ugly one to your left and this bucket of snot standing right in front of me. Cousin, you take out the other cretin to your right with the cauliflower ear."

Suddenly, all four Yankees swiveled to take the measure of Jack who they hadn't seen up until now. You could almost hear their eyeballs clicking in their heads. Jack had decided his first corpse would be the jellybean right in front of him. Then he would take out the one to Gerard's left. Mr. LaRue hadn't drawn a firearm yet, and although he undoubtedly would, it would be too little, too late to save himself.

Mr. LaRue collected his composure, tugged on the lapels of his coat, smoothed the wrinkles in the front of his shirt now that the tables were turned on him and his demise was a forgone conclusion unless he thought quickly. He didn't want to lose face in front of his lackeys. He said, "Come on boys. We'll settle this score later. Mr. Twyman, you just signed your death warrant, same as your sneaky cousin here behind me."

Gerard said, "Not so fast, Mr. LaRue. Why put off for another day, somethin' that's better done right now? I'm ready to die to defend my property. Are you prepared to die to steal it? Let's settle it oncet and for all. I wanna dance right now!"

You could see the fire in Gerard's eyes. The hired help knew instinctively that he meant every word. Fortunately Mr. LaRue did, too. He shouted, "Wait! Wait! Wait! I was a mite hasty. You don't have anything we need or want. You're just a measly, pissant operation! Stay out of our way and we'll let you live! Come on boys, let's go."

Gerard retorted with venom in his voice. "Mr. LaRue, it's me lettin' you and these three peckerwoods live and don't you never forget it! If'n I see you or any of these jaybirds again, you better fill your hands with iron because I won't hesitate. I will drop you all where you stand and leave your bodies for the vultures to pick clean. The coyotes will gnaw on your bones. Now get outta here while you're still able to breathe."

The Yankees piled into the Packard in haste and without decorum and rushed away in a cloud of dust. Once they were gone, Gerard said, "Jack, would you go fetch Mabel? When you get back we'll head straight to Falstaff's. I'm loaning you twenty bucks so you can buy that .38 Smith and Western and a box of ca'tridges. If'n lead had started flyin' today, I ain't sure I'd still be vertical. You pay me back whenever you can. No rush. I'll check the house and the other buildings whilst you're gone."

"Thanks, Cousin. Much obliged. For what it's worth though, I had you covered like Stonewall Jackson at the First Battle of Manassas. I'd 'ave mowed these Yankees down like hay durin' harvest before they could even load their britches. I bet that skunk standin' right in front of me already did. Did you get a gander of the look on his face?"

Gerard grinned.

Jack responded, "Be right back. Tulip and Mabel are both sorry they missed this comeuppance."

Chapter 7:
The War on Nerves Goes Full Tilt

Gerard and Jack got a move on. They didn't allow any 'moss to grow under their feet.' At the same time, they were alert, fully aware that the Yankees might be at Lonesome Corner doing a slow burn over their collective humiliation. If that turned out to be the situation, there was bound to be blood in the street.

They plodded along and finally arrived. Praise the Lord! Neither the sidewinders nor their big fancy machine were anywhere in sight.

When Gerard and Jack entered the general store, they made a beeline for the gun counter. The .38 was still there but Mr. Falstaff had sold out of .38 caliber bullets. He said he had placed an order for .38s plus a variety of other calibers but didn't think they would come in for a couple more weeks. Gerard and Jack both thought that was an optimistic assessment but they didn't comment.

After a long pause, Woodrow stated, "All righty then. Seems like everyone's on edge right now. I ain't the onliest store which has run out of cartridges but it just ain't right to sell a gun without at least one box of bullets."

He sent his wife, Clarabelle, upstairs to their residence. She returned with a box of Western brand .38s. Mr. Falstaff said, "I carry a .38. I always keep a few boxes on hand for personal use.

Right now, you need these worser than me. Price is the same as for the Peters. That will be $2.50."

While they were waiting for Clarabelle to return, Jack decided he needed a holster and a cartridge belt. He bought a Denver-style leather holster and a canvas duck cartridge belt with 24 leather loops. He had to pony up $4.80 out of his own pocket in addition to the twenty bucks his cousin had loaned him. Jack loaded the revolver, filled the cartridge loops, and put on the rig while Gerard commenced conducting his own business.

Gerard bought a half-case of forty percent (nitro glycerin) dynamite sticks, meaning a dozen, plus a small wooden box containing a dozen blasting caps, in addition to twenty feet of fuse cord. Cost him almost eight bucks.

Mr. Falstaff asked, "Gerard, why you want all this dynamite for?"

He replied, "I have some pesky rodents I haven't been able to get rid of through conventional means. Desperate times call for desperate measures. I'm sure this is way more than I actually need but I don't want to have to take time to come back for more if'n I'm wrong."

"Well just remember you gotta store it in a dry place and it only has a shelf life of about a year before it starts leaking and gets really dangerous."

"I know. I bought me a half-dozen sticks a couple of year ago. Needed to blow some stumps. I ain't forgot how to use it. We'll be careful. Always are.

"By the way, you had an influx of out-of-staters recently?"

"No. We get the occasional vehicle from West Virginia ever so often. Mostly trucks hauling coal. You know that. You've seen 'em.

"We did have an automobile from somewheres else though, now that I think of it. From Ohio I believe. Stopped here for fuel a day or so ago when I was by my lonesome. The missus and younguns was down to the church helping set up for a social.

"A big, black Packard. New, I'm pretty sure. Shiny. Four pompous, dandy sorts travelin' in style. One of 'em come in and bought a ginger ale and three Coca Colas. Didn't say much. Give me a twenty to pay for eight gallons of gasoline and four soda pops. Rang up a sale for $1.76. I asked for something smaller. He got all huffy and said it was either a twenty or a fifty. Darn near cleaned out all my singles because it was early in the day and we ain't had many customers."

"How's come you didn't ask if he could check with one of his travelin' companions to see if'n they could make change?"

"Because he was a big unpleasant-looking feller. Nose was flattened across his face. Had a long scar next to his eye and a cauliflower ear. A professional boxer for sure. Tell you the truth, he give me chill up my spine. I didn't want no trouble. I was glad when they drove off. Why you askin'?"

"Woodrow, them's the guys who was waitin' on my verandah today when we come back from runnin' some errands. Told me I was goin' to work for them in the liquor business. Threatened to kill me and Jack if we didn't."

"Oh, dear Lord! What did you do?"

"Well, we seen them afore they seen us so I had Jack sneak up behind 'em with that twelve-gauge of his and threaten to kill 'em first. Jack was so close to two of 'em afore they knowed he was there, he'd 'ave blowed 'em into mincemeat plus ventilated that shiny new machine of theirs. They skedaddled but I'd be a dern fool to think that was the end of it.

"By the way, I'm askin' you to keep this to yourself. Don't tell nobody. You tell your woman and it'll be all over Clifford. That's just the way it is. If'n these jaybirds do come back and somethin' bad should befall 'em, I don't want Sheriff Harned to come nosin' around my property. If'n Cousin Jack and I quit comin' 'round after a week or two, you might have someone stop by to see if'n we're still alive.

"Oh yeah. I don't want no one findin' out I bought no dynamite nor Jack buyin' that new revolver. Agreed? This could mean the difference of us livin' or pushin' up daisies or even goin' to jail just defendin' ourselves. God forbid it should ever come to that. Tell me we are agreed and let's shake on it."

Woodrow stuck out his hand. Both Gerard and Jack shook it in turn. Woodrow said, "As God is my witness, I won't tell a living soul about this. And Gerard, Jack, the two of you keep an eye out. Don't take no crazy chances. If'n I do hear or see somethin' I think would be useful, I'll let you all know."

"Thanks. We're obliged to ya. Come on Jack, we gotta go. We still got things to do afore we call it a day."

It was dusk before they arrived at the farm. They slipped in the back way like Jack had done earlier to avoid an ambush. No one was lurking. Deep down they didn't think there would be, but it was no time to take chances. Mr. LaRue hadn't had enough time to gin up a foolproof plan yet or recruit additional hired guns. He might even have to run it by his boss before taking retaliatory action.

The Yankees had to have a decisive and overwhelming victory over Gerard to scare all the other hillbillies into utter compliance. At least that's what Jack and Gerard thought. They hadn't heard of anyone being beat to death or burnt out yet.

Today, Gerard and Jack had set themselves up to be the abject examples of what happens to hillbillies who refuse to toe the line. Besides that, there was a thing called revenge. Gerard and Jack understood that concept very well. In hillbilly-speak, it was called having a feud. Mr. LaRue absolutely needed to punish Gerard and Jack for the humiliation he suffered in front of his thugs who were too stupid to understand anything except brute force. They would lose respect for him otherwise.

Yep. As sure as God made little green apples, a brutal showdown was in the works. If Mr. LaRue allowed today's defiance to go unanswered, he would have to tuck his tail and slink out of Lawrence County in shame. Suffer the consequences sure to come at the hands of his boss. He would be done. Finished.

'Forewarned is forearmed.' Gerard and Jack would be ready.

Chapter 8:
Up Jumps the Devil

The rest of the week was tense. Jack had moved his all his belongings and the cot out to the barn. He didn't go to the outhouse without taking his revolver. Neither did Gerard.

They established a new pattern. Since Jack was already in the barn, he fed all the animals, milked the cow, mucked the stalls, and collected the eggs. Gerard made breakfast. Every other morning they took care of the farming. Tended the crops. Weeded and watered the garden. Anything else that needed doing within the confines of the curtilage. They checked the telltales and the still everyday, sometimes twice a day. They delivered milk and eggs to Falstaff and elixir to drop sites. So far, so good.

It had been a week-and-a-half since they distilled Jack's first batch of moonshine. They netted seventeen gallons. Business had picked up. Maybe folks were worried about a shortage. The Yankees were still making their presence known by threats and intimidation and by twisting arms. Even so, nobody had been kilt, nor had anyone been burnt out yet so far as they knew. The other issue firing up folks was paying a buck-and-a-half a quart for elixir. Undoubtedly some had already done so. They just weren't admitting it. Too ashamed.

Rabbit Bluff inventory was up but nevertheless it was time to distill another batch. 'Make hay while the sun shines,' as it were. If trouble came to them, they might well be out of operation indefinitely. So, on Friday, which also happened to be the last day of the month, they mixed three more barrels of mash. Although everything related to farming and distilling was operating better than it ever had, life was nerve wracking due to their concern about hostilities evolving into a shooting war with Mr. LaRue and his henchmen. It was the proverbial calm before the storm.

Saturday night while Gerard and Jack were sampling their wares, one might even say taking pride in their work, they decided Gerard would go to church in the morning by himself. Truth be known and sad to say, it was more about gleaning the most up-to-date information from the hillbilly grapevine with respect to the Yankees than it was about worship. Gerard was a church member but Jack was still just a visitor. He hadn't decided yet if he wanted to join or not so his absence would not be as noticeable as Gerard's, plus he had the trust of most of the congregation. Jack was too new to have earned it.

Jack would stay at Rabbit Bluff and check the telltales. He would go on foot today with good reason. Afterwards he would remain in the woods on watch, ensconced in an old sycamore tree along a ridge which was about four hundred yards away from the still. This was in the area Gerard surmised would be along the most likely route a trespasser who was unfamiliar with the terrain would take, especially if he wanted to sneak into Clifford and onto Rabbit Bluff 'through the backdoor.'

Gerard expected the interloper(s) would come in from the west on Oxmoor Trail, which was a pretentious name for a narrow goat path that cut off from the Ashland-Paintsville Road roughly halfway between Louisa and Ulysses. It dead-ended at Clifford. They knew the Yankees had purchased fuel at Maynard's Ashland Oil and Garage along that route so they were probably aware of this passage.

The plan was this. After church, Gerard, mounted on Oscar,

would enter Rabbit Bluff from the woods road which cut through Mr. Mac's property. He would check for machines parked in the woods on or near Rabbit Bluff. If things were all clear, he'd pick up Jack and they would check the mash before heading back to the house.

Truthfully, since Sunday was the Lord's Day and a day of rest, they didn't believe Mr. LaRue would risk a reconnaissance of the farm and/or destruction of their still on a Sunday, simply because farmers would normally be at rest, not preoccupied with work and thus quicker to respond to a threat.

Also, Gerard was convinced that to be successful locating the still, Mr. LaRue would need a local turncoat to guide him through the woods. Gerard couldn't imagine the city slickers embarking on a search and destroy mission in the woods all on their own. It would be too easy to get lost or detected or snakebit. They'd need help. And if Gerard figured out who the snitch was, 'Katy bar the door!' The rat would be fortunate to survive the wrath which would befall him and not just from Gerard, either! The rest of the community would exact revenge, too.

It was about ten o'clock. Time when most Baptist churches were just limbering up for a righteous sermon on hellfire and damnation. (Salvation was a topic usually saved for Easter and Christmas. Must keep the congregation scared straight!)

Not having a functioning watch at the present, that was Jack's estimation of the time he first spotted a trespasser. From his perch on high, he could see a far piece in three directions even though all the trees were nearly in full foliage. One became two and two became three until he counted nine trespassers altogether. Mother of God! This could go bad for him if he wasn't careful.

Only one trespasser was dressed in farm clothes. This had to be the rat. Jack didn't recognize him, but he could see that the guy was tall, rail thin, with a dark beard extending down to his chest. Gerard would probably know who he was.

The rest were city slickers. The portly one was definitely Mr. LaRue. The rat was carrying a shotgun. Nobody else was carrying a long gun but you could bet your bottom dollar they all had a sidearm, maybe two. A couple of the unwelcome guests were toting satchels. It could be their lunch or it could be explosives. Maybe they just wanted to catch a copperhead or two to entertain the family and they needed a safe container to carry it home. Take your guess.

It was obvious by the way they gaggled together, gesticulating in several different directions, which suggested they couldn't reach a consensus in their confabulation and couldn't agree on where to search first. Jack could see they had split into two groups. Before long, both groups were lost to his sight. They weren't headed directly towards the still but sooner or later, he knew they'd figure it out or inadvertently stumble across it.

Jack decided he would have to get on the ground and track

them. Figure out a way to divert them if they were getting too close to the still. Thank God the mash was covered and just in the early stages of the fermentation process, otherwise they'd be able to smell their way straight to it.

Jack shimmied down the tree, unslung his shotgun, and trotted in the direction that he had last seen the trespassers headed. He made very little noise. Here and there he stopped to check for a footprint or a broken twig or anything to confirm their direction. He could see they were on a trajectory to bypass the still which was off to the left, but he worried that they'd circle back around and find it. Then things turned serendipitous for Jack, or maybe not, depending upon one's perspective. Most folks believe that 'all's well that ends well' but is that really true?

Jack slithered down a ravine and started to climb up on the other side. He raised his head just enough to peek over the top to see what he could see. What he saw were city slickers taking a breather not more'n fifty yards ahead. One was Mr. LaRue, himself, who was wheezing like his chest had been crushed by a raging buffalo. Two were palookas he had seen at the farm. He'd never seen the fourth one before, but the fourth one saw him and sounded the alarm. "Look it youse guys! One of them hicks is right behind us!"

All but Mr. LaRue jumped up and slapped leather. (Mr. LaRue was struggling to get up, as awkward as a turtle which had been turned upside down on a fencepost by a kid who was tormenting him.)

Jack ducked back down in reflex and surprise, but he popped right back up with the shotgun shouldered, cocked, and ready to fire. The man who spotted him was out well in front of the others. He fired at Jack with a Government Model Colt .45. Four shots in all. His shots were way off the mark, all passing over Jack's head. It didn't necessarily mean he was a bad shot. It meant he was too hasty because he was running full tilt and Jack presented a low profile, hugging the ravine with only his head and shoulders exposed. When target number one got to within thirty yards, Jack sent a load of number four buck down range into his chest. He dropped like a hundred-pound sack of oats falling from a hayloft.

Next up, was the palooka who had been nearest Jack the day of the confrontation. He was the one who nearly soiled his trousers when he turned around and saw Jack pointing a shotgun at this chest from a distance of only fifteen feet. This hired gunman was pointing a long-barreled revolver at Jack but he had yet to fire. Must have been waiting to get closer for the perfect shot. Unbridled rage filled his eyes. Jack shot him in the neck and face right after he passed his dead cohort. He too, went down without a whimper. Jack needed to reload the shotgun but he didn't have time.

The third pursuer stopped in his tracks about twenty yards away. This was none other than old Cauliflower Ear! He fired two rounds from a revolver at Jack. He shot wide to the right. Jack returned fire with his new revolver. It was the first time he ever shot it. He aimed center of mass and fired three rounds. Jack knew he had hit the thug at least twice but nevertheless he didn't go down. Dern! Old Cauliflower Ear was attempting to line up another shot but his arm was just shaking too much.

Jack would have emptied the rest of his cylinder in an effort to completely vanquish this son of Satan but he was all out of time. Mr. LaRue was standing behind the wounded Cauliflower Ear, shouting and waving his arms like a spinning windmill in a windstorm at the other four gangsters and the skeleton-like traitor behind him, screaming for them to murderlize Jack forthwith. All five were running pell mell in Jack's direction, intent on doing just that.

Jack decided discretion was the greater part of valor. He scrambled out of the ravine and ran for his life back towards the sycamore. He ejected the empties in the shotgun and put in two fresh loads while he ran.

Jack could hear his pursuers shouting encouragement to one another while cursing him with vile threats as they pursued him. They were gaining. He knew he was about to be overcome by an overwhelming force. He would never be able to get them all before they got him. He was seeking a place with good cover to hide and make his last stand but he couldn't find anything suitable. At best, he had another minute before they all converged on top of him. He could drop two, maybe three, but there were six of them left. One or two of them was bound to get lucky.

He muttered to himself, "Oh Lordy, it's times like these I wisht I was a rabbit again, even if it was just for thirty minutes."

Poof! He found himself nibbling on a bit of clover under a blackberry bush.

Within seconds the remaining gaggle of rampaging trespassers had run right past him and then began circling back, led by the local traitor. Jack saw that he was about forty years old. He was a popeye. His left eye was canted left and maybe just slightly upward. He was swearing like a drill sergeant whose platoon of recruits had just tumped over the outhouse while the General was voiding his bowels.

Everyone except Mr. LaRue was searching high and low. They were determined to find Jack and obliterate him, but Mr. LaRue wanted them to clobber the directions to the still out of him first. He even offered a fifty-dollar bonus to the man who located Jack first! He also told the traitor that he wouldn't be paid one red cent if they didn't locate the still.

They milled around and crossed right in front of him so many times that Jack began to worry they wouldn't leave before his thirty minutes were up and he became human once again. He began hopping back in the direction of the still to put some distance between himself and them. If they even noticed him, they paid him no mind.

Then his circumstances changed again.

Circumstances changed for Gerard, too.

Chapter 9:
The Cavalry Arrives

Gerard didn't remain one minute after church to collect intelligence. He had spoken with Armand MacDougal briefly before the worship service began. Armand said Marvin Gibbs was supposed to be distilling for the consortium now but he didn't know of any others who were. Armand also said he heard the Yankees was supposed to be looking for Clyde Higgins and Gerard.

Fortunately, the worship service was called to order before it became necessary for Gerard to respond. The unasked question and his unanswered response prompted him to bug out before the question came up again. He didn't want to put his personal business out there on the grapevine. That, plus he was a little worried about Jack being all by his lonesome in this time of strife.

Gerard cut through the woods on his way home. It put him in the general vicinity where he expected trespassers would park their vehicles for concealment to be close to, but not on Rabbit Bluff property in the event of detection.

Sure enough, two machines and a brown mule were parked exactly where he thought they would be. First, he examined the mule carefully. It was about fifteen years old. It had an old Army McClellan saddle on it. He didn't recognize it. As such, he still didn't know who the stoolie was but by George he'd find out today!

He recognized Mr. LaRue's Packard but not the Maxwell. They looked just like invasive, metallic rodents to him. Manmade woodchucks. By golly, that's exactly what they were! Desperate times call for desperate measures, indeed. Besides, the hidden machines meant that Jack was probably in serious trouble. He would have to hurry. If he were too late, it could be 'all she wrote' for Jack.

Gerard tethered the mule a hundred yards away, deeper into the woods but on his own property, not Mr. Mac's. Then he returned to the machines. He tethered Oscar close by. He dug into his saddlebags and retrieved two sticks of dynamite. He cut off two one-foot lengths of fuse. He used his knife to cut a hole in the top of each stick. He inserted each fuse into a blasting cap. Then he inserted a blasting cap into the hole of each stick.

He opened the gas cap on both vehicles. Then he placed a lit stick of dynamite on the back floorboard of each one. He mounted Jerome and trotted back to the traitor's mule. He untethered it and smacked it's rump. It galloped away towards the north, probably headed straight for home. Then Gerard rode Jerome as fast as he would go east in the direction of the sycamore tree.

Dern! Jack was not there. Gerard arrived just as the first automobile and then the second exploded. Even from his current position the sound was deafening. He could see black smoke rising above the tops of the trees.

Gerard hobbled Oscar behind the sycamore. He took his rifle and jogged about fifty yards farther east where he took up a prone position under a cedar tree surrounded by bushes, aiming in the general vicinity of his still. Then he waited.

It didn't take long. The first man he saw was his old neighbor, Wilbur 'Dirty Bill' Conard. Son of a gun! So Dirty Bill was the snitch! Gerard let him pass. He would get him later. Suddenly, he had a change of heart. He set his rifle aside and grabbed his .32 caliber revolver. Gerard decided to punish Dirty Bill but not kill him, so he shot him in the butt where all his brains and character were located.

Dirty Bill screamed like a rabid hyena and fell down like he had twisted his ankle in the worst way. Gerard smiled as he watched. Dirty Bill moaned as he struggled to stand back up. He hobbled in the direction of the explosion, no doubt looking for his mule. He didn't even bother to look for his assailant! Guess he was too scairt to find out who shot him but most likely he already knew.

Gerard thought, "What a hoot when Dirty Bill discovers that his mule ain't where he left it. Lucky for him, or otherwise the mule would have paid the ultimate price for Dirty Bill's sins. Too bad. Wilbur had a painful walk ahead of him. He deserved it, and much, much more."

The next trespasser was one of the hoodlums who had been to Gerard's house. Gerard sent a .30-30 round into his heart. He collapsed like he'd been knocked out in the final round of a boxing match, never to rise up again.

Gerard saw two thugs he'd never seen before. He dropped the closest one with a shot to his throat. The other one stopped like a frozen statue before turning around and skedaddling back in the direction from whence he came. Gerard shot him in the back and laid him out, arms stretched wide like he was hanging on a cross, except he was lying face down.

Gerard waited a full five minutes just like you do after you shoot a deer to give it a chance to bleed out. Nobody else came along. He didn't know how many trespassers there were. He knew Mr. LaRue was bound to be here someplace, hopefully already shot dead by Jack.

Where the heck was Jack? Did they kill him?

Gerard inserted three rounds into the tubular magazine of his rifle, topping it off. He unhobbled Oscar, mounted, and began cautiously making his way towards the still. He had to find Jack! He'd kill the other hired guns if he came across them.

He came to within a hundred yards of the still and stopped. He listened and watched for ten minutes. His sixth sense was pinging. Crickets. No sign of friend or foe. He was about to move on when Jack suddenly appeared before him from behind a big oak.

"Jack! I thought they got you! I been lookin' high and low for you. Are you okay?"

"Yep. I got two of the gangsters who was in the yard the other day, plus one I didn't know. Not for sure if I kilt old Cauliflower Ear or not. Then they started to swarm me so I had to find a place to hide. I was hoping they'd split up but they didn't. I saw the rat. He's got a popeye and a long beard. I also saw Mr. LaRue. I think he must've gotten away. There was four thugs I didn't recognize."

"Well I got three myself, including one who was at the house. I shot the rat in his backside. I let him get away a purpose. All I wanted to do was mark him so he couldn't lie his way out of it. I reckon that means two, maybe three including Mr. LaRue, got away."

"I reckon so. They're probably on Mr. Mac's farm by now. Want to track 'em?"

"Nope. Did they find the still?"

"No, but they were within a hundred yards. They'd probably 'ave found it if I hadn't stumbled onto the three I shot, plus Mr. LaRue. First their focus was on me. Then their focus was on the explosion. Then I reckon their focus was on you and now it's on getting away."

"Jack, I want you to ride Oscar back to the barn. Saddle up Tulip. Bring the horses and plenty of rope and a couple of canteens of water. We got five or six bodies we need to disappear. I'll look around here checkin' for survivors. You'll hear it if I find 'em. Understood?"

"Understood."

The rest of the afternoon involved putting the bodies of six trespassers on the backs of Mabel and Jerome and carrying them farther into the woods to the deepest ravine. They had six bodies so it took three trips. The only thing they stripped from the bodies were their firearms and extra ammunition if they had any. The thug with the Government Model .45 had a spare magazine so they took it, too.

Altogether, they collected the .45 Government Model pistol, three Smith & Wesson revolvers, two in .32 caliber and one in .38, two Colt revolvers, one in .32 and the other in .45 Long Colt. They also netted ten rounds of .45 ACP, 21 rounds of .32, three rounds of .38, and five rounds of .45 Long Colt. They stockpiled these weapons and ammunition in the cave where they stored the moonshine just in case they would be needed 'for a rainy day.'

Once they had the bodies laid out single file in the ravine, Gerard shoved sticks of dynamite into holes he poked into the walls on both sides of the ravine about eight feet apart and about four feet from the bottom. He lit the fuses and skedaddled fifty yards away. The detonation caved in dirt and rocks over all the bodies, burying them a whole lot faster than it would have taken Gerard and Jack to dig unmarked graves. They hoped the detonations didn't arouse the curiosity of their closest neighbors, who might decide to investigate or ask questions. Even after the explosion, the ravine was still remote and deep. If it were left alone for a year, no one would ever suspect it was a gravesite.

Afterwards, they rode back to where the automobiles were parked. Parts were scattered everywhere. Both chassis were burned out hulks. Gerard knew that in a day or two, these blown up machines would net him a visit from the law. They needed to get their stories straight.

That night they took hot baths, ate like ravenous buzzards, imbibed a taste or two or maybe three, of smooth, hundred-proof elixir, and slept like pacified babies.

Chapter 10:
Dealing with the
Aftermath and Forging Ahead

They didn't have any visitors on Monday. Good news. It was unlikely the explosions went unnoticed so that meant nobody was in a hurry to get in the middle of Gerard's business. Best 'to let sleeping dogs lie.'

Tuesday morning Mr. Mac stopped by. He was riding his pet Appaloosa, Teddy, named for former President Theodore Roosevelt. Mr. Mac hadn't been a Rough Rider, but he did fight the Spanish in Cuba in 1898 as an activated private in the Kentucky National Guard. President Roosevelt was his hero. He asked, "How you boys doin'?"

Gerard responded, "We're hangin' in there like a hair in a biscuit. How 'bout yourself?"

"Fair to middlin'. I seen a couple of blowed up automobiles on my property up near the woods road. You fellers wouldn't know nothin' about that, would you?"

"Maybe. Can't say for sure. Saw 'em myself the other day. Must've happened whilst I was in church. Wouldn't want the law to come snoopin' around blamin' me since my cabin is the closest one to where they got blowed up. Any idea who they belong to?"

"I 'spect they belong to them Yankees who been nosin' around tryin' to corner the liquor market. I figure they crossed the wrong fellers and got what was comin' to 'em."

"I bet that's it, then. They shouldn't 'ave been trespassin' wheres they don't belong an' tryin' to muscle honest, peace-lovin' folks. I say good riddance to 'em. What say you?"

"Agreed. If they was the fellers from Cincinnati, my guess is their outfit will be comin' around lookin' to even the score. Bein' that some folks claim you all got the nearest still 'round these here parts, they'll probably fix the blame on you. Wouldn't surprise me none at all if they come around next time with three or four machines jam-packed with gun thugs. Burn you out. Leave you and Jack laid out like you was a giant-sized pair of dead mackerel used for target practice."

"Wouldn't surprise us neither, if'n they tried. 'Course, me and Jack ain't goin' down without a fight. It'll cost 'em dearly if'n they do come."

"Heck, I know that, but you all is good neighbors. The best. I'd hate it if'n somethin' bad happened to you all."

"We'd hate it, too. Sheriff Harned come to see you yet?"

"Nope. My guess is he don't know nothin' about it. I doubt those peckerwoods would 'ave said anything to him. What do you reckon?"

"What I reckon is, there's a songbird in cahoots with 'em who might be singin' like a yellow-bellied warbler. One of our own,

who'd show these gangsters where our rig is if'n he could find it.
A tall skinny feller with a long beard who lives 'bout two miles
north of us. Ya see, Jack here, he had a dream 'bout it. In his
dream, this feller got shot in his backside when he was trespassin'
on another man's property. He was leadin' some city slickers to
where he thought a still was located. If'n it was the low-down cur
dog I suspect Jack was dreamin' about, and if'n the dream come
true, this miserable snake-in-the-grass just might be inclined to
concoct some story and run to the sheriff expectin' some kind of
satisfaction."

"Gerard, I got a good idea who that skinny feller is. He ain't
nothin' but no account white trash. He'd sell out his mother for a
dollar. No, a half dollar. I doubt he'd run his mouth though, that
is, assuming Jack's dream did turn out to be true. Squealin' like a
bitch in heat would have serious repercussions for him and his
whole dern family. They'd have to skedaddle acrost the river to
West Virginny or Ohio or someplace else. I wouldn't lose no sleep
over him."

"Prob'ly so. Mr. Mac, you got any idea where them Yankees
lay their heads at night?"

"Well, how far up the totem pole you wanna go?"

"All the way up to the tip top. If'n the owners of them burnt
up cars was after me, I'd like to know a little more about 'em. See
how much trouble I could be facin'. I figure since you get around
a lot more than I do with all your business connections and
whatnot, you might have a better idea than me."

"Well, the really big dog is this pharmacist feller who also
happens to be a big shot lawyer. His name is Mr. George Remus,
Esquire. You might 'ave read about him in the newspaper. He
lives in Cincinnati. I heared he figured out a way to beat the

government at its own game. This part of the story is kind of funny. Listen to how he done it.

"When the legal distilleries went bust 'cause of the Volstead Act, Mr. Remus bought up many as he could for a dime on a dollar. They's a loophole in the law what allows doctors to write prescriptions for folks to buy alcohol for medicinal purposes but the catch is, you can only buy one pint a week. Being this Mr. Remus is a druggist, he knowed all these doctors who would write prescriptions for a small profit without askin' no questions so he was off and runnin'.

"I heared he owns fully operational breweries which is all strictly illegal now. He's also got registered distilleries makin' bonded whiskey for medicinal purposes, which is legal, assumin' it's only sold to pharmacists; howsomever, he also owns distilleries which ain't registered no more what are makin' illegal whiskey on the sly. On top of all that, now he's decided to corner the moonshine market.

"Man thinks he's bigger than the Chicago mob boss, Johnny Torrio. I 'spect he'll learn otherwise someday that he's more like Big Jim Colosimo, who got too big for his britches and just got hisself whacked by somebody in Johnny Torrio's outfit. Greedy swine wants it all! The whole shebang! In just a few months, Mr. Remus become one of the richest men in America, right up there with the Rockefellers and the Carnegies. The law can't touch him, or so it seems.

"I also heared he's smarter and a more crookeder lawyer than any prosecutor ever thought of bein'. Smarter, anyway. Maybe not crookeder. When Mr. Remus was practicin' law, he specialized in gettin' cold-blooded killers off who was charged with murder. Done a lot of them cases for free or next to nothin'. Now them killers is beholden to him. Snaps his finger and they come a runnin'. Got a small army of 'em at his command. Anyone gets in his way, that's it! They wind up bumped off. No witnesses or at least none what's willin' to testify. Charges get dropped if'n anyone was even charged to begin with, which ain't often. Simple as that! Wham! Bam! Thank you, ma'am!

"You know, they always was a bunch of thievin' inbreds up there in Northern Kentucky. A regular Sodom and Gomorrah and now they's all in cahoots with Mr. George Remus. He's got Newport and Covington and Kenton County and Campbell County sewed up. They all works for him - judges, prosecutors, sheriffs, police chiefs, speakeasies, casinos, you name it. He's got his fingers in every pot which makes easy money but mostly in alcohol.

"Recently he started spreadin' his reach south and east. Ever'one knows the best whiskey in America is made right here in Kentucky. Mr. Remus has someone on his payroll callin' the shots ever'where he's set up business, plus enforcers to keep ever'one in line. The crooked politicians answer to these Yankee bosses who set up shop in their counties. I don't know who all these bosses are, but the one in our county is this smooth-talkin' weasel named Mr. Elgin LaRue, a crooked, washed-up boxing promoter who brung in a bunch of thugs with him. He prob'ly works for someone higher up in Ashland, who prob'ly works for somebody even higher up in Newport, who answers directly to Mr. Remus, hisself. Catch the drift?"

"Yep. So do you reckon Sheriff Harned or Judge Durham or the Commonwealth Attorney, Mr. Livingood, kowtow to Mr. LaRue?"

"Mebbe, but I don't think so. Not yet anyways. Can't say for sure about any other county exceptin' for the ones up close to Cincinnati. Of course, Mr. LaRue's henchmen claim they got ever' county up and down the line all sewed up in their hip pockets. No doubt they got some but I question if'n they really do control all the counties surroundin' us like they says; however, they prob'ly will in time if'n someone don't run 'em off first."

"So do you know where Mr. LaRue set up shop?"

"Well that's an interestin' question. When Mr. LaRue first showed his face in Lawrence County, him and his whole crew was stayin' at the Dixie House Hotel on Main Street in Louisa. You know where that is. It's the swankiest place there is from Covington to Ashland to Pikeville, if'n you're goin' that far.

"In the beginnin', these sidewinders tried to impress folks with their fancy duds, expensive machines, fat wallets, and phony big city manners but it didn't last for long. 'A leopard don't change his spots.' Them hoods started runnin' roughshod over folks unchecked and wide open. They was loud, rude, boisterous, flauntin' their flasks of bonded whiskey and their sidearms, swearin' somethin' awful in public, escortin' drunk floozies throughout town in broad daylight and such as that. They even had their hands on the bottoms of some of 'em whilst they was paradin' 'em up and down on the sidewalks.

"The sheriff started gettin' complaints from the onliest ones who could complain without gettin' kilt - the old, dried-up, blue-haired, self-righteous church biddies. You know who I'm talkin' about - the Women's Christian Temperance Union and such as that. Not even the preachers spoke up. Too scairt. Tucked their heads and kept on walkin'. These hellfire, always complainin', teetotalin' old biddies ain't the kind of folks the gangsters could buy off, nor the kind they could beat up, nor bump off without creating a storm they couldn't weather. Mr. LaRue and his entourage was just about to get run outta town by the sheriff and some silent, influential, dangerous fellers in his inner circle afore they could set up permanent shop."

"What influential dangerous fellers?"

"You know I'd tell you if'n I could, but I can't so don't ask. If'n you really want to know, find out who the big donors are for his election. Think about who's done been accused of killin' someone but nothin' never come of it 'cause the person kilt had it comin'. Go back a few years. That's all I'm gonna say. And they's more'n one. They's all quiet, in the shadows, and dangerous. One of 'em even done time in West Virginny for shootin' a feller but that was years and years ago and ain't many folks what knows about it. If'n I had a life-threatenin' situation, these is the kind of fellers I'd want on my side.

"Now I don't know if'n the sheriff's crooked, but if'n he is or

he ain't, he couldn't survive for very long if'n he let hooligans get away with runnin' roughshod over ever'body and the law itself, 'specially where folks can see it for theirselves plain as the nose on your face. Sheriff Harned's job was on the line. Somethin' had to give and it did.

"Mr. LaRue wised up real quick after he had to bail a couple of his palookas outta jail. That cost him a hunnert bucks. Then he had to pony up two hunnert more in fines. They was convicted of drunk and disorderly, simple assault, and indecent exposure."

"What on Earth?"

"Oh, yeah. These wise guys started a ruckus in the hotel lobby with a scaredy-cat, thumb-suckin', fancy pants, confectionary drummer from Louisville name of Delmar Doolittle right in front of God and ever'body. Called him all kind of foul names, slapped him upside the face several times, pulled his hair, th'owed his hat on the floor and stomped on it, poured whiskey all over him, but the worst thing they done was when they stripped off his trousers and drawers and all his duds and exposed his private parts to ever'one present. I'm surprised ain't no one mentioned that to you."

"Oh my gosh! I can't even imagine it. People must 'ave been embarrassed to death for him and scairt to death for theirselves to keep quiet about it."

"You're dern right they was. Bet Mr. Doolittle don't never come back here again! Right after that episode, Mr. LaRue and his gang up and moved outta the Louisa city limits and rented Sawyer's Roadhouse on the pike like you was goin' to take the ferry over to Fort Gay in West Virginny."

"Yep. I know exactly where that's at."

"Yeah, well due to Volstead, Sawyer's was just about out of business. Folks dance and kick their heels up a lot more if'n they's well-lubricated. Sawyer's always had a little prostitution goin' on as a sideline but you can't mask it when the booze, food, dancin' and ever'thing else dries up. Then it's just a bawdy house, no longer a restaurant with a saloon.

"The church ladies was all up in arms raisin' Cain, wantin' all them hussies run outta town, actin' like they had a whole dern harem. Heck! It was only six or seven and not ever' night. Sheriff Harned didn't have no choice. This was before the Delmar Doolittle incident, too. He couldn't let things ride. He had to raid Sawyer's to silence waggin' tongues if'n he wanted to get hisself re-elected, 'specially now that women can vote in the next election due to the 19th Amendment. God Almighty! What's become of this world?

"One night the sheriff hauled both Matilda Sawyer and Belinda Jenkins off to the hoosegow when he knowed for certain they both was in the act of doin' what they do best - satisfyin' their customers. Ha! Charged 'em with lewd behavior - that sort of thing. Made 'em pay a fine and scairt off two of their best customers who was afraid of gettin' exposed, no pun intended. A couple of staunch Baptists so I heared. One of 'em a deacon, too. Business dropped off to a trickle.

"So, when Mr. LaRue and his bunch showed up, Matilda was more'n happy to rent him the whole shootin' match. Course, she and Belinda stayed on to clean and cook and handle private matters for a little extra on the side I'm sure. Folks still has to get their ashes hauled. Not only that, Mr. LaRue has access to bonded whiskey and I know the ladies appreciate that. They can get away with it too, so long as they stay private and don't take in no outside customers."

"That sounds like someone's always there day or night."

"I'd 'spect so. How's come you to ask?"

"Just wonderin' that's all. You know how many men and machines he's got?"

"Well, I know they was at least four machines but two of 'em is all blowed up now. Plus they got a utility truck for haulin' product. They's at least ten, mebbe a dozen strangers workin' for him in Lawrence County. I don't have no idea if'n he has men in any other county."

"How you know all this? Nobody I ever talked to has this much knowledge about Mr. LaRue or his thugs."

"Well let's just say I am well acquainted with one or two of the fallen angels who's been affiliated with Sawyer's Roadhouse off and on over the years. Get my drift?"

"I do. I've been at a loss of consortium myself ever since Francine passed away, and I thunk about makin' a pass over thataway onecet or twicet. I surely do miss female companionship but I ain't ready to get hitched again. Heck, I ain't met a female since Francine that strikes my fancy. She prob'ly set the bar too high. Besides that, then I'd hafta kick old Jack out and he's a good worker and a fine companion."

"I certainly understand. At my age, a visitation ever' other week suits me to a T. Boys your age is usually more randy than a gentleman such as meself."

Jack interjected, "Mr. Mac, do you know when Mr. LaRue delivers a load up north or where he takes it?"

"I heared he goes oncet a week, usually on Wednesday and always late at night. They's a clever bunch. They drive it to

Ashland and load it on a boat. Less likely to get hijacked than takin' it overland."

"You think they store it in the barn at Sawyers?"

"Can't say for sure. Prob'ly. I do know they always have two fellers at or inside the barn. Wherever the stash is, you can be assured it ain't settin' in plain sight unattended. What's on your mind, Jack? I can see your wheels a turnin'."

"Well, it's been two days now since their automobiles got blown up. Wouldn't surprise me none to hear that some of their hired killers got kilt themselves whilst they were sneaking around. I'm thinking they might be short-handed right now.

"Also, I do believe you're right. They blame Cousin Gerard and me. They gotta make an example outta us to get everyone else in line. Me? I'd rather play offense instead of defense. Got more options that way. Wonder what they'd do if they lost a load. Suppose it got hijacked or blown up. What you reckon would be their response?"

"My guess is they'd show up right here at Rabbit Bluff with a whole platoon of hired guns. Besides that, they always have one car followin' the load and most of the time another one leadin' it like an Army convoy, only smaller, with at least four gangsters riding shotgun.

"Jack, these guys is hired to fight. They's all itchin' to pull a trigger. You ain't gonna buffalo 'em into surrenderin'. Sheriff Harned would come down on you like the Wrath of God if he thunk you was goin' all Hatfields and McCoys on him."

Gerard jumped back in. He said, "Mr. Mac, Cousin Jack is right. If 'n we don't take the fight to them, they'll show up here in the middle of the night with more guns than we could fend off. We'd be 'deader than a doornail' and nothin' would ever come of it. You know that.

"We gotta come up with a way to turn the tables on 'em. It's the onliest way to protect ourselves. Plus, we gotta run 'em outta the county. Do the sheriff's job for him since it don't look like he's up to it. As it is, dangerous friends or not (and I bet they're all long in the tooth) he's only got two deputies. Bevis Bottoms is a complete screwball even if'n he is the sheriff's son-in-law, and Dwayne Turley is eighty years old if'n he's a day. The sheriff's on his own. These mobsters is way outta his league."

"What do you propose? Whatever you do will have to be all or nothin'."

Jack responded, "We need a dozen men, more if we can get 'em. They have to have a 'dog in the fight' and 'grit in their bellies.' If they don't have everything to lose, they won't be motivated to see it through to the end. They might chicken out or squeal on us.

"This is how we do it. We find a desolate stretch of the road that ain't too close to a house. We topple a tree and use it as a roadblock. If they get that far, the gunmen in the first unit will have to get out of their machine to move the tree. Problem is, the other thugs may not get out and we wan't 'em all out, even the men in the truck.

The roadblock is just a back-up because we get us a couple of buckets of roofing nails and scatter 'em in the road a quarter-mile or so before they get that far. Hopefully, each car will get a flat or two before they get to the roadblock and have to stop anyway.

"We all come a horseback so we can travel through back trails and the woods so as not to get seen going or coming back home. All of us wear masks during the assault and take long guns. Pistols would just be for back up. The idea is, we want to be beyond their effective range so none of us gets hurt. We split up into two groups, one on either side of the road. We tether or hobble our mounts inside the tree line well out of sight and harm's way. Otherwise, it's a long walk back home but at least we don't get any flat tires.

"When they stop and get out of their vehicles, we pick 'em off. Nobody gets away. Nobody. Absolutely so mercy. Black flag. That's why each man's gotta have real grit. When the fight's over, we blow the truck hauling the shine. Then we fade into the woods and every man goes home. We all keep our mouths shut; otherwise, our gooses are cooked. We don't want anyone on the ambush if he can't do this without going all soft in the head. Who we pick is the most important part of the plan if we want to be successful.

"This is Tuesday. We need to do this tomorrow night. Mr. Mac, you don't need to go with us, but we sure could use your help recruiting trustworthy men."

Gerard said, "Jack, you sound like you done this afore."

"Let's just say I learnt how to do a lot of things in the Army that I didn't ever do before I was in the war. Didn't think I'd ever have to do 'em again, but I never encountered a passel of thieving, murdering, hoodlums trying to take over our livelihoods either."

Mr. Mac said, "Count me in. Ever'thing you all said is true. This here is a good plan. I'll go talk to Lige Bostick and Adrian Pullman. Lige has four growed sons. I'll also talk to Rufus Claiborne. He's a tough old coot. Him and his son and son-in-law also operate a still. I'll also bring the nails."

Gerard said, "I've got the dynamite. We'll also bring axes. I'll talk to Reuben Clark and T.R. (He goes by T. Rex) Tapp. Also

Bloody Gene Whalen and his sidekick, the Duke of Hazard, Herschel Wilson, hisself. They's all in the business. T. Rex has a ten-barrel rig which he operates with his son and  nephew. Ever' one of 'em will stand and fight."

Jack asked, "Where do we set the ambush? Also, where and what time do we meet tomorrow night? What do you all want me to do while you all are out recruitin'?"

Gerard replied, "You hold the fort down here. God forbid they come back today."

Mr. Mac also replied, "There's a burnt-out house on the east side of the Ashland Road about four miles north of Louisa. We'll meet there. I don't think LaRue's crew leaves Sawyer's Roadhouse afore midnight and prob'ly not until one or two. Just to be safe, we should meet there at ten to give us time to cut down a tree, pick teams, and set up. Tomorrow will be a long day and night. I'll stop by this evenin' to confirm we're still good to go. Talk to you all later."

"See ya."

Chapter 11:
Crossing the Rubicon

Wednesday morn, Gerard and Jack were up well before daylight. Jack even woke up the rooster! They had about twenty miles of back trails to travel and eighteen hours to get there by rendezvous time. They didn't expect to return before daylight tomorrow, assuming all went well. They put out extra feed for the animals, turning out all the four-footed creatures except for Tulip and Oscar into the pasture. They left the henhouse door open. They hadn't seen a fox in over a month and hoped none would come around during their absence. Ditto for coyotes.

Both men brought along a slicker, rope, axe, blanket roll, two canteens of water, jerky and hardtack, and of course their weapons and extra ammunition. Gerard packed his last two sticks of dynamite with fuse and blasting caps. Theirs was a no-frills war party.

This had to be done, and done now, but it came at a bad time. The mash had fermented. It was time to distill more elixir but that had to be shoved to a back burner. Their very survival depended upon annihilating their enemies while they were short-handed and unprepared. Shock and awe. If they could blot these thugs out and vanish without a trace, maybe the Yankee handlers up north would decide Lawrence County was too bloody a venue to be profitable. Otherwise, this would be a long, drawn-out, grisly affair just like the Hatfield and McCoy feud which still lingered to this day with bitter feelings on both sides after fifty years.

It turned out to be a pleasant day with a cobalt blue sky and only a few, puffy white clouds. The temperature ranged from mid-fifties to low-seventies with moderate humidity. This was indeed a fabulous day to be alive in their perception of what the Garden of Eden must have been like.

Throughout the morning, Gerard and Jack rode in silence along lonesome roads and back trails without coming face-to-face with a living soul. Around noon, they stopped along the Tug Fork of the Big Sandy River to take a break, smoke their pipes, and rest the mules. They were refueling on their Spartan rations when T. Rex Tapp and his son and nephew happened by.

The Tapps came very well prepared as one might expect of a man with his means. T. Rex was mounted on a handsome sorrel stallion. He was carrying a ten-gauge, Winchester lever-action shotgun and wearing a holstered Colt .45 Peacemaker. His son, Barton, was mounted on a bay gelding. He was carrying a Springfield, bolt-action, .30-06, plus he was wearing a full cartridge belt with a sheathed Bowie knife. T. Rex's nephew, Matthias, was riding a pinto mare. He was a mountain of a man. He was packing a .45-70 Henry lever-action rifle and he was wearing crossed bandoliers filled with cartridges. The Tapps weren't out hunting for small game. They were all loaded for bear.

They decided to stop, too. T. Rex had a coffee pot and the fixings. Jack made a small fire and a half-hour later everyone enjoyed a stout cup of steamy coffee. T. Rex also opened a jar of blackberry preserves and a poke full of biscuits which he generously shared. When all were sated and it was time to move along, they parted ways so as not to arouse the interest of any passersby. Seen as a group, there could be no mistake that they were expecting trouble.

Gerard and Jack thought they made good time. They arrived around eight. The others, which included everyone on their wish list except for Lige's son, Erath, who was down with a fever, were already there. It was obvious the group came highly motivated because they had already chopped down a lightning-struck cottonwood to use as a roadblock. Altogether, they were sixteen determined, fed-up, hillbillies focused on the mission to exterminate a passel of pit vipers.

It was soon evident that this gathering of citizens from all across Lawrence County, plus scores of their neighbors who were not invited tonight, all had their bellies full of Yankee interlopers with their imperious attitudes and the strong-arm tactics they employed to seize control of the county and more particularly, its sub-rosa moonshine industry. They always show up unannounced in wolf packs at family farms to terrorize and overwhelm folks when they have no support from kith nor kin. The law was either too weak or too scairt to stand up to 'em. Heck, maybe the law was even in cahoots with 'em! For sure these Yankees had spies in their hip pockets, fingering which farmers had stills and which ones would be most likely to fold.

One example of Yankee transgressions mentioned, was the story of Adrian Pullman's cousin, Cecil G. Benge, who had been beaten senseless by four Yankee thugs when he refused to go to work for them. He was still recovering. Not only that, they chopped up his still, stole all his inventory, and threatened to kill him and his whole family if he didn't have a batch ready for them by the end of the month. Cecil swore revenge but he couldn't make it tonight due to his injuries.

Another egregious example they expounded upon was

Hiram Duckworth. Two machines full of Yankee bandits ran him off the road when he and his son, Junior, were delivering a load to his wholesaler in Louisa. (Nearly everyone there knew Hiram had a sweet deal. His wholesaler was his brother-in-law, Ike Alexander, one of the conductors on the L&N. Ike kept thirsty passengers with a half-dollar to spend, well-lubricated with a pint of Hiram's elixir to help while away the miles as they rocked back and forth along the rails.)

Two Yankees held Hiram at gunpoint while another robber clenched Junior in a headlock, and fourth one with a cauliflower ear ran a straight razor a little too close acrost his throat, giving him a slight cut almost ear to ear. Then he sliced Junior's shirt and bib overalls completely to shreds. Left him standing in his red union suit.

They stole Hiram's product, 180 pints in all, and then they slashed all four tires on his REO truck. They said from then on, Hiram was working for them or he and his whole family would wind up kilt, burnt up in their house some night when they was all asleep.

Everyone had a story and some had more than one, so Gerard and Jack shared theirs, including the part about the untimely demise of Cauliflower Ear and five of his associates. What Gerard deliberately failed to mention, in the unlikely event a snitch was in their midst, was where they buried the bodies. Talk is cheap without proof and there is no proof if there are no bodies. Nevertheless, the entire group erupted into cheers when they learnt that the ambushers got ambushed and that a total of six were now feeding the worms, having passed on into the next realm to meet their Maker. No doubt they were all shoveling coal in the pits of Hell for all of Eternity.

Understanding now that Mr. LaRue's gang was probably reduced to half-strength, the assemblage was heartily emboldened with one hundred percent in concurrence that they wipe out all remaining gangsters tonight with special emphasis on Mr. LaRue, himself. Black flag rules. Have no mercy. Take no prisoners. Leave no witnesses. Eradicate the influx of Yankee predators.

They also vowed to tar and feather Wilbur Conard if he hadn't already flown the coop and any other traitors they could identify. Lige Bostick's son, Darnell, said his wife's cousin told her that Dirty Bill and his family up and moved to Fayette County to be closer to his mother-in-law. That resulted in boisterous guffaws and numerous derogatory comments about lying weasels in human form.

When everyone settled down, they split up into east and west groups. Gerard, Jack, Mr. Mac, T. Rex, his son Barton, his nephew, Matthias, Bloody Gene Whalen, and the Duke of Hazard Herschel Wilson were in the eastern group. Lige Bostick, his three sons, Adrian Pullman, Rufus Claiborne, his son, and son-in-law were in the western group.

At eleven o'clock they pulled the cottonwood across the road. They waited until midnight to scatter sixteen pounds of roofing nails on the road in an effort to spare the tires of an errant, innocent late night traveler, of which they had none.

The horses were tethered or hobbled well inside the tree line on both sides of the road. Each man took up his position, most of them prone or behind some cover wherever they felt they could have the most effect without exposing themselves to harm's way unnecessarily. Levi Bostick was the youngest and the most wiry. He clambered up in a towering oak tree to be the lookout. Then they waited, each man alone with his thoughts.

The sky was partially cloudy but the moon was nearly full. The temperature was in the high fifties. The wind was slight but it was sufficient to keep the mosquitoes away. It was a perfect night to do what had to be done.

Chapter 12:
Hillbilly Justice

When a person is keyed up, ready for battle, anxious, sorting out the cosmic events which brought him to an imminent, seismic event of life versus death, even ten minutes seems like an eternity. Actually, the wait this night was only forty-five minutes from the point the nails were scattered. Mr. LaRue and party were early.

Levi Bostick shouted out the alarm before shimmying down the tree but they all could see the headlights coming from the south. When the gangster convoy was about a half-mile out, they could distinctly identify three sets of lights.

Jack could feel his heart starting to pump faster, adrenaline coursing through his veins. His shotgun was double-cocked and ready to fire but this battle was against Yankee gangsters, not German soldiers. Does it really make a moral difference, fighting for self and family instead of the flag? Then after the fact, dissecting who shot first to assess blame or to justify self-defense?

If you happen upon a copperhead crossing your path, do you concern yourself about letting it strike first before you kill it?

Is it unworthy to sucker punch a bully twice your size before he mops up the floor with you? Take him out by surprise before he can marshal his superior strength.

Didn't someone say, "God created all men, but Samuel Colt made them all equal?"

Which is more important - abiding by Marquis of Queensbury rules or survival?

Without a doubt, Jack subscribed to the philosophy that there are no second-place winners in war, whether it is a war between individuals or a war between nations.

Why was he even having these thoughts? He and Gerard had already killed and planted six of these sidewinders!

In his heart of hearts, he knew why.

When Jack went off to war, he didn't know any Germans. None. They had not done a single thing to wrong him personally. He did not hate them. What he did do, is love America. He assumed Germans loved Germany.

That all changed on his first trip to the front line with the onset of incoming artillery barrages. They were terrifying. He never saw the artillerymen who fired the barrages which nearly killed him, but thereafter he imputed their homicidal behavior to all German soldiers. He hated German soldiers collectively but not individually. Then that changed too, the moment a German soldier impaled his best friend in the platoon on a bayonet. Jack emptied every round in his rifle into that demonic savage. From then on, Jack couldn't wait to kill more German soldiers. From then on, he was the demonic savage.

Those homicides were all sanctioned and even encouraged by the U.S. government to help win the war. The gangster deaths on Rabbit Bluff were not sanctioned, although they probably would have been exonerated after a jury trial, but maybe not. One never knows how a jury will rule. Neither Gerard nor he wanted to find out, so they disposed of the bodies without notifying the law. That would probably seal their fate in a jury trial were it to come up now.

So tonight, in just minutes, this coterie of Lawrence County citizens of which he was one of the informal leaders, planned to wipe out all the remaining Yankee gangsters preying on Lawrence County, assuming they all showed up. Leave the bodies where they lay to send a resounding message to Mr. Remus or anyone else who wants to seize control of the county or their individual, unlicensed, untax-paid liquor businesses. This is the Land of the Free, Home of the Brave. No more tyranny!

What is the proclamation on the yellow Revolutionary War flag, otherwise known as the Gadsden flag - the one with the coiled rattlesnake? Isn't it 'Don't tread on me?'

Dont Tread On Me

The uninvolved citizens of Lawrence County would either support these actions tonight or they wouldn't. Time would tell.

The die had been cast.

So, this was why.

The first car in the procession was a Studebaker open touring car. It got its first flat tire as soon as it rolled over the farthest scattering of nails. It continued another twenty yards or so when the next three tires burst. Then it came to a screeching halt.

Next in line was a White utility truck. It blew two tires, but because it was traveling too close to the Studebaker, it didn't come to a complete stop until it rear-ended the Studebaker with a resounding crash.

The last vehicle was a Stanley Steamer, four-door passenger sedan with an enclosed roof. It stopped well behind the truck with only one front tire blown.

It was as if Time took a pause for about thirty seconds. It took a few moments before all the gangsters realized the danger confronting them. Then the Stanley Steamer began to maneuver in an effort to turn around and flee. When the driver paused to shift from reverse to first gear, it was as if all Hell broke loose. All vehicular motion was stopped by a hail of bullets coming from both sides of the road. For a split second, someone returned fire from the passenger side of the vehicle. Steam escaped from the radiator but none of the occupants did.

Nearly simultaneously, two occupants bailed out of the **Studebaker.**

The right front seat passenger had a Thompson submachine gun. He stopped about two feet from the vehicle. He let loose with an entire, fifty-round drum magazine, but he hit nary a soul. In fact, it was doubtful he could see any of his intended targets, all of whom were concealed and most of whom were prone, including Jack; however, all the men on the east side of the road could see him.

Jack was a scant fifteen yards away. He waited for this assailant to quit spraying bullets. Then he let the machine gunner have both barrels of number four buck.

Jack wasn't the only person to shoot him, either. So did Mr. Mac and Gerard with their Winchester rifles. Others probably did, too. In the aftermath, this thug resembled a pile of ground hamburger weighted down by about six ounces of lead.

The right rear seat passenger stepped out of the car firing a Winchester Model 12 shotgun. He made it three feet from the vehicle before he also dropped dead from lead poisoning. The senior Tapp and his son got credit for this kill.

The driver of the Studebaker fell before he exited completely out of the vehicle. He took a headshot from Lige Bostick with multiple assists from other shooters.

Initially, the left rear seat passenger remained seated in the vehicle but being an open touring car, it didn't provide much cover. Then he stepped out, also firing a Thompson submachine gun but he only managed a half-dozen shots before he shuffled off this mortal coil, perforated like Swiss cheese.

The driver of the truck tried to put it in reverse but he too, suffered head shots - two of them. Most of his head was missing. You couldn't make out his face. His own mother couldn't have recognized him. Both of Lige's older sons took credit.

The passenger of the truck jumped out firing a from each hand like he was Butch Cassidy or the Sundance Kid. You got to give him credit for panache. He made it six feet before he dropped like an anvil falling from the sky, credit taken by Bloody Gene Whalen and the Duke of Hazard.

In less than a mad minute of concentrated gunfire from the roadside and sporadic, unaimed gunfire from the motoring gangsters, the epic Lawrence County Shootout came to an abrupt halt.

Most of the victors ran up to the Stanley Steamer to see who was in it and if there were any survivors. All had perished. There were 68 bullet and buckshot holes in the vehicle itself. The driver and front seat passenger were unknown names although both were recognized by Rufus Claiborne and a couple others. Both gangsters had holstered revolvers. Another Thompson submachine gun with a fifty-round drum magazine was laying on the front floorboard.

The abhorrent Mr. Elgin LaRue, Satan in the flesh, was sprawled out across the back seat and floorboard. He was riddled with bullet holes, but the one between his eyes was exceptionally gratifying for all to see. He had a nickel-plated, .38 caliber Colt Lightning revolver in his hand. One round had been discharged, identifying him as the lone shooter from this vehicle.

Only one of the Lawrence County participants incurred an injury. Adrian Pullman stepped on a nail but the sole of his boot was so thick that the nail barely broke the skin. Somebody, but not anybody there at this time, would be pretty busy picking up nails for the next several days if they didn't want to injure their horses or suffer more flat tires.

The informal, unsworn militia left all the bodies and the cars where they came to rest except for the driver of the truck, whom they pulled the rest of the way out of the doorframe and left lying on the road. They placed all the gangster firearms in the bed of the truck, which also contained 172 gallons of shine.

They decided not to blow the truck. Instead, they poured the moonshine all over it and set it on fire. The idea was to destroy all the moonshine and the gangster guns. They wanted the sheriff and any other passersby to get a good look at the Yankees and to see just how well-armed they were.

Jack had picked up his spent shell casings. He recommended

that the others do likewise, just in case the sheriff or anyone else decided to conduct a thorough investigation. He said, "If you shoot a .44-40, why advertise it? Maybe have the law nosing around asking what caliber of gun you own and what brand of ammo you use. It don't prove anything, but why include yourself in the pool of possible suspects?"

Around 2:30, after Gerard lit the truck on fire, they broke up and headed their separate ways home through the woods and the back trails. They wanted to be long gone before anyone stumbled across this battlefield.

Gerard and Jack needed to get back to their still but it wasn't going to happen today. They'd been up for nearly 24 hours and they had a long ride ahead of them.

They arrived mid-afternoon. The four-legged critters and the chickens were all alive and unmolested. Praise the Lord! They tended to Oscar and Tulip first. Everyone got an extra ration of grub. The four-legged ones got brushed.

Gerard and Jack dined on country ham, pinto beans, green onions, canned peaches, and biscuits, washed down with cool, crystal clear, limestone-filtered water.

They closed the day out on the verandah, smoking their pipes, and sipping on elixir. They cleaned their firearms in the light of the moon while they were thus engaged. They discussed the events from the past two days.

Gerard said he was dying to know what the sheriff was going to do regarding the nine dead gangsters.

He also said he was glad they didn't blow the truck because it would have led the sheriff straight to Rabbit Bluff, blown up vehicles not being a common occurrence. Nobody would be dumb enough to believe that two incidents of exploded vehicles in the same week was a coincidence to be blithely dismissed.

Finally, he said he was proud to have been involved in the eradication of Yankee vermin from Lawrence County and that every citizen who fought there was a true-blue patriot.

Jack concurred. He suggested they dare not ask too many questions once word got out. He hoped it would be reported in the Ashland Telegraph. Find out what folks who hadn't been afflicted by the gangsters were thinking. Would they be horrified or would they be relieved?

They both hit the rack before the sun eclipsed the horizon.

Chapter 13:
Waiting for the Other Shoe to Drop

Friday was a busy day. Gerard needed to make his milk and eggs run. They also needed to drop off elixir at the various woods rendezvous sites. They didn't want to alter their routines, giving anyone pause to wonder if they were part of the gangster massacre. Best not to confirm any suspicions. They also couldn't afford to let their guard down in the event Mr. Remus decided to burn Lawrence County to the ground like Sherman did to Atlanta.

After tending to the animals, Gerard went to Falstaff's and Jack made the stump run, as they referred to it, tending to the elixir drop-off sites. They also planned to run off a few batches of shine in the afternoon assuming that the mash was not ruined.

They had an abundance of milk and not a few eggs. Gerard took the wagon, pulled by Jerome and Mabel as usual, but this time he brought his rifle which he hid under a gunnysack on the floorboard under the seat. He didn't feel comfortable relying on his pocket pistol if things went all Hatfields and McCoys on him.

Woodrow was happy to see him. He was running short of fresh milk and he could never have too many eggs on hand. After they transacted their business, making Gerard two dollars and fifteen cents richer, Woodrow asked, "You hear about the shootin' Wednesday night on the Ashland Highway up north of Louisa?"

"Jack and I been busy. What shootin'?"

"Big one. Nine fellers was kilt. None of 'em local. They was transportin' a load of shine. One of 'em was that Yankee boss named Mr. LaRue. They say it looked like the Battle of Perryville, exceptin' there wasn't no dead horses nor mules - just dead Yankees."

"What's Sheriff Harned think?"

"I heared he wasn't makin' no big fuss over it but our worthless, meddlin' governor, Edwin P. Morrow, hisself, heared all about it and got his panties in a wad, thinkin' this might be another hillbilly feud like the Hatfields and McCoys, so he's sendin' some special investigators over here to make sure Sheriff Harned don't sweep this under the rug. They's supposed to arrive on the Monday afternoon train."

"Governor Morrow is a sorry sapsucker. He's one of the weak-kneed politicians who favors the Volstead Act. You can't never trust no black-hearted Republican!"

"Nope. Well, I'm just glad you and Jack wasn't caught up in it. The governor wants to hang some pelts on the wall. (Poor choice of words.) I heared altogether they's six special investigators who's s'posed to turn Lawrence County upside down and inside out until they catch the ones what done it."

"Didn't you say these was all outsiders, prob'ly from Ohio, if'n they was with Mr. LaRue? That don't sound like no hillbilly feud to me."

"Gerard, Governor Morrow is from Somerset in Pulaski County down in Southern Kentucky near Tennessee. He don't know nothin' about how things is done in Eastern Kentucky. The main thing you gotta know is, he's a Prohibitionist and he hates moonshiners. 'A word to the wise is sufficient if the wise is sufficiently wise.' Get my meanin'? I bet those special investigators will be crawlin' up the bunghole of anyone ever suspected of makin' a quart of shine, okay? Tread lightly."

"We will. Appreciate the tip. What about Mr. LaRue's bosses? Heared if they're comin' down to try to settle the score?"

"Nope. I ain't heared nothin' about 'em. If they heared the special investigators is comin', they might wait until they see how that all plays out. Don't poke a hornets' nest while they's all buzzin' around. Prob'ly not a concern right now for anyone what lives here. Course, it would be interestin' to see how them jaspers would fare if they tangled with the governor's men.

"Hey! What's that I hear about some blowed up cars bein' found on Mr. Mac's place? I heared they both belonged to Mr. LaRue's crew."

"Yep. It happened while I was in church Sunday mornin'. Someone told me Wilbur Conard was involved, but I can't see that peckerwood blowin' up no fancy machines."

"Well, he didn't, or so I heared. I heared he was leading a bunch of Mr. LaRue's men on a wild goose chase lookin' for a still on your property. I also heared he got his backside shot when he was runnin' away. Seems like I sold some dynamite just afore that happened but I just can't recall who it was."

"Well, whoever done that, I'm sure he had his reasons. Besides, someone said Wilbur and his family up and moved away. I 'spect that situation done took care of itself, Mr. LaRue no longer bein' a member of the livin', or so you say. There ain't nobody left to file a complaint."

"That's right. Wilbur done moved to Fayette County so I was told. The sheriff come out to talk to you or Mr. Mac about it?"

"Not me. I don't know if he spoke to Mr. Mac."

"Well, I reckon it's not an issue then. Praise the Lord! I don't want none of my neighbors and friends to have no trouble with the law."

"Me neither. Well okay then. Guess I better get back to my chores. Give my best to the missus. Bye."

"You bet. Same to Jack."

Jack had a profitable morning, too. Gerard told him to take extra jars on his rounds since they missed making a run on Wednesday or Thursday. Sure enough, Gerard was right. Several sites had two dollars stashed in jars. One had three. Oscar, who was some kinda mumped up about bein' the pack mule instead of the ridden mule, had been loaded down with thirty quarts when Jack set out. Last stop was at Old Man Bailey's, who took all six quarts Jack had left in his pannier. When he was done, Jack had $28 and two hundred pounds of oats to show for the day.

Gerard arrived home first. He ate a quick lunch of leftover biscuits and sausage. He left a note for Jack to meet him at Roscoe's. (Roscoe was his code name for the still.)

When Jack returned, he noticed that Mabel was grazing in the pasture so he turned out Oscar. He grabbed some jerky and refilled his canteen with water. Then he rode Tulip over to the still.

When Jack arrived, he saw that Gerard was already cooking mash in the distilling pot. He asked, "How was the mash?"

Gerard responded, "A little old. We may not get as many jars this batch. We'll need to work all night to get ever'thing done."

"What's the rush?"

"Governor Morrow the Moron is sendin' six special investigators to catch the hillbilly moonshiners what kilt the gangsters, who he apparently thinks are from a competing hillbilly clan. Governor Morrow's a teetotaler so his men are s'posed to root out all the moonshiners in Lawrence County who done this. They's s'posed to be comin' in on the train Monday.

"We gotta cook this batch and break down the still and hide it with our stash. We gotta eliminate all evidence that a still was ever here. I'm bringin' the hog down tomorrow to help the mules eat any mash residue. We gotta smooth over any trails. Woodrow thinks they plan to search the property of all suspected distillers. Looks like we'll be outta business for awhile. I'm pretty sure they ain't got no right to do that. Ain't they gotta have a witness and get a search warrant or sumthin'?

"I'd say we take a powder out of Dodge until they's gone but we got the animals to tend to. I'll stay behind like nothin's happened but I suggest you pack your gear and camp out on Mr. Mac's property. Take Tulip. I'm sure he won't mind if'n you ask him. Besides that, they's unlikely to search his property since he ain't a known moonshiner.

"Take a dozen jars with you. Better load up with grub and take plenty o' tobaccy. You might be there for a month. We don't want nobody layin' eyes on you and we don't want to be beholden to Mr. Mac. If'n you run out, I'll bring you some more.

"If'n they already know you been livin' here, I'll tell 'em you went to North Dakota to visit your sister. What're they gonna do if'n they can't find you - take away your birthday? I bet these so-called investigators couldn't find an Eskimo in Alaska even if'n someone drew 'em a roadmap."

"It's okay by me either way. I feel obliged to stay but I may be of more help in the woods. Remember, neither the Yankees nor you could find me when I was in hiding. I can keep an eye on 'em if they do show up and I guarantee they'll never know I was there. That being said, I am a little concerned they might go down into the ravine where we buried those fellas."

"We'll need to check. If'n we have to, we can take a pick and some shovels and dump more rocks on top of 'em. Consider this. We have some time. We won't be the first farm they search. We should know afore they get to us whether they's city slickers, searchin' on horseback or afoot, if'n they know what they's doin', and if'n they have local guides. My guess is they won't.

"It'd take a couple of months for six investigators to do a thorough search of the whole dern county. My guess is, they'll do like most folks and go for the low-hangin' fruit. Pass on the apples up at the top of the tree. I doubt the governor will give 'em more'n a month to make a splash in the papers. They'll prob'ly arrest some dunce for makin' shine who wasn't even there on Wednesday night. I ain't too worried they'll catch any of the fellers who was there but if'n they do, them boys sure as Hell won't squeal."

They had a plan and they set their backs to it. They finished the last run at three o'clock the next morning. They went back to the house to rest and recharge their batteries. They'd pick up where they left off in the afternoon.

Chapter 14:
Making Hay While the Sun Shines

The rooster didn't give a hoot that Jack and Gerard had been up half the night. He started crowing at daybreak and didn't shut up until Jack rolled out of his cot and scattered the scratch.

All the creatures wanted to be fed. The cow needed to be milked. The mules and horses needed to be brushed and the stalls needed mucking. 'No rest for the weary and the wicked don't need none.' Everyone on a farm has to work like a Hebrew slave. Even the two cats, Samson and Delilah, were hard at it catching mice in the corn crib after they cadged a few squirts when Jack was milking Matilda.

Life on a farm has a rhythm and it seldom bodes well if one ignores it. There's a symbiotic relationship between Man, the animals, and the plants, even the ones that are unwanted such as pests, predators, and weeds. To ignore Mother Nature is to put everything in jeopardy. The rooster was just reminding Jack and Gerard of their responsibilities and pushing them to get the lead out.

After breakfast, Gerard put a rope on the hog and led it to the still. Jack led the horses. The animals ate all the spilled mash and trampled the earth around the still until the sodden ground resembled a pig sty or a feed lot. They even licked as much of the inside of the mash-soaked barrels as they could get to.

Gerard and Jack cleaned the pot, coil, and barrels in the creek. Then they moved the whole assembly into the rear of the second cave as far back as they could because they could still smell the residue of mash from what had seeped into the staves. They brushed away their tracks from the cave entrance and even added some big rocks in front of it. When they were done, it was concealed even better than it had been the first time Jack saw it.

They finished their chores by checking the ravine. From the top it looked just fine but they trucked all the way to the bottom just to be sure. All was well. None of the deceased had risen from the grave. Gerard and Jack both doubted that anyone would make his way all the way down to the bottom looking for a still that one could clearly see from the top just wasn't there. Even if they were searching for a corpse, they would have to be well motivated to go down there simply because the climb up and down was arduous to man and beast alike.

They spent all day Saturday tending to the garden. Sunday they both went to church.

The congregation was buzzing about the Lawrence County Massacre. Brother Hayslip preached against the evils of demon alcohol. Jack noticed a few squirmy parishioners but he knew that for the most part the sermon fell on deaf ears.

After the service, the congregation set up some tables and folding chairs in the yard under the shade trees and feasted on fried chicken, sugar cured ham, potato salad, fresh greens, homemade bread and butter, cole slaw, sweet pickles, strawberry preserves, grape jelly, apple butter, apple pie (there were five to choose from), carrot cake, cinnamon rolls, oatmeal cookies, fresh milk, sweet tea, and of course, coffee. The church ladies outdid themselves and though it was appreciated by all, none more so than the bachelors and widowers, with special emphasis on Gerard and Jack.

Nobody mentioned the massacre in the presence of the preacher or the womenfolk but it was the only topic on everyone's mind. There were all sorts of theories and speculation galore on who might have been involved. None of the names mentioned to Gerard were involved. It was said that Sheriff Harned had been asking questions of the women at Sawyer's Roadhouse, as well as to a few of the suspected moonshiners up north near Louisa, but apparently no one had any information.

They were all concerned about what the special investigators would do when they showed up in town tomorrow. The long and short of it was that the parties unknown who had been involved in the massacre were keeping their mouths shut and maintaining low profiles. This was extremely frustrating to Mr. and Mrs. John Q. Public because folks like to exalt their heroes and vilify their villains. To Gerard and Jack, this was fabulous news. Nobody knew diddly squat.

On the way back from church, Gerard said he was going to Louisa so he could eyeball the special investigators. He'd leave today with the wagon and return on Tuesday most likely. He wanted to know what they look like so he would recognize them and to size them up. He wanted to know their names. He wanted to know if they were city slickers. He wanted to find out if they would be in automobiles or on horseback. He wanted to see what types of weapons they were carrying. He also wanted to know what type of reception they were receiving from the sheriff and the public.

This was a reconnaissance mission, plain and simple. At the same time, he would go to Ellicott's Mercantile and stock up on a few things Woodrow Falstaff didn't carry or was out of, not least of which was ammo. Maybe get some more canned peaches, raisins, common crackers, jelly, etc. He said he'd see if they had any small tents for Jack. If not, he would buy some canvas and rope and some stakes. Gerard would spend the night at Spellman's Livery Stable.

In the meantime, he suggested that Jack stop by Mr. Mac's with a jar of elixir to see if it was okay to camp on his property. Assuming it was, scope out a few promising sites. Gerard also needed Jack to make the milk and eggs run and to service the drop sites.

Jack said for Gerard to consider it all done. Then he asked Gerard to pick up a copy of whatever newspapers were available. Also, a couple of cans of Prince Albert smoking tobacco. Agreed.

After Gerard left for Louisa, Jack rode over to Mr. Mac's. His daughter, Farrah, son-in-law, Hubert, and four grandkids were all visiting from Pikeville. They were busy cranking ice cream on the front verandah and they invited Jack to help. It was a special afternoon for him, socializing with an energetic, happy family.

It had been a long time since he had been around children or anyone not an adult male for that matter, who was carefree, joyful, and having some fun. He thought it might be nice to have a wife if she were pleasant, and not fixated on trying to change him into someone he was not - like a teetotaler or a non-tobacco user or someone who went to church every time its doors were open. Maybe someday.

Eventually, he had an opportunity to speak to Mr. Mac in private. Mr. Mac said he was happy to have Jack roam around on his property. Old MacEwen's Farm, his own pun on Old MacDonald and E-I-E-I-O, was 546 acres, most of it wooded. He said Jack could stay in his house, use the barn, or anything else he needed. He said he did not think the special investigators would try to search his property since he wasn't known to be a distiller; however, now that Jack brought it up, he decided to speak with Hubert, a lawyer who mostly handled wills and civil matters, but also the occasional criminal case, to see what his options were. Of course, legal or not, it wouldn't prevent someone from trespassing and Mr. Mac would be glad to have Jack out there to put the kibosh on the likes of that.

Jack thanked him but said he planned to stay in the woods. He might need to use the barn on occasion since he would have Tulip, or in the event the weather turned off bad, like a toad strangler or tornado or such.

Matter resolved, Jack went back to socializing, gobbling down two bowls of ice cream, and sharing a little nip of elixir with Mr. Mac and Mr. Hubert McCoy (of the famous McCoy clan) while he and Mr. Mac smoked their pipes and Hubert smoked his Havana cigar.

Today, all was well in the Land of Eden.

Chapter 15:
Gerard Gathers Intelligence

Gerard strolled into downtown Louisa Monday morning a little before noon after he completed all his purchases. He positioned himself on a park bench across the street from the Louisville and Nashville railroad station in front of Carmichael's Hardware Store. He selected this location so he could quietly observe the passengers disembark from the 1:20 train, which was due to arrive from the Kentucky capital in Frankfort by way of Lexington and Ashland. He whiled away the time smoking his pipe and perusing yesterday's newspapers from Louisville and Lexington and today's paper from Ashland.

The two bigger city papers were filled with lurid, gory details. The Louisville *Journal* hypothesized that this was the beginning of a moonshine war between two warring big city gangs, perhaps from Chicago or Cincinnati or even Baltimore. It was noted that the license plates on the vehicles were all from Ohio, suggesting that the Ohio gang was wiped out by the other big city gang. It also mentioned the Thompson machine guns recovered in the burnt truck and the number of bullet holes in the Stanley Steamer. It suggested that the investigation should be turned over to the Federal Bureau of Prohibition.

The Lexington *Star* opined that this was a battle between two opposing mountain clans, similar to the McCoy and Hatfield feud in bygone days. It didn't mention the Ohio license plates or the submachine guns or bullet holes. It claimed that local law enforcement was not up to the task of apprehending the killers and bringing them to justice. Finally, it cited an inflammatory statement by Governor Morrow that moonshining was a major problem in the mountain counties where it had been ongoing since the eighteenth century by uneducated, recalcitrant residents. It said he was sending a team of crack investigators to track down the killers.

The Ashland newspaper surmised that this was a lethal fight over territory between an outside organized crime syndicate and a local moonshine empire. Cub reporter Elijah F. Quigley, only 21 years of age and a recent graduate of Centre College in Danville, as well as the new hire at the *Telegraph*, hypothesized that the convoy had been ambushed by locals who were very familiar with the area and who possibly had an informant within the ambushed gang. He pointed out that there did not appear to be any deaths from the faction which ambushed the convoy.

Sheriff Harned stated that none of the decedents had been positively identified yet by next of kin, photographs, or by the latest and most modern investigative method to confirm a person's identity. He was referring to the comparison of fingerprints of unknown subjects with fingerprints on file of known subjects at police departments and sheriff's offices. This is absolutely the only irrefutable way to verify a subject's identity since fingerprints are unique to each individual. It's a scientifically proven fact.

Unfortunately, this method is always a long shot. First, the requesting agency needs to determine in which city or county they believe the unknown subject might have been arrested.

This is a big ask. It's a lot of work for the receiving agency, and to make a request too frequently is to get refused with regularity. Think of the 'boy who cried wolf' once too often.

Second, the requesting agency must mail a set of fingerprints (and photograph if they want to cover all their bases) of the unknown subject to the other agency and wait for them to respond. It could take weeks and even then, most replies are negative.

 Third, not many law enforcement agencies maintain an organized, comprehensive, arrestee fingerprint filing system. To do so, they must employ a fingerprint expert, who examines and classifies the fingerprints of all the agency's arrestees into the three major types (arches, loops, and whorls), and records each print in a specific order (the right thumb being number one and the left pinky being number ten), and then annotates this classification sequence on the arrestee's Bureau of Identification (B of I) card, said cards being maintained in alphabetical order. (The examiner looks for a classification number in his file that matches the exact classification number of the unknown subject. If he finds a match, then and only then, he pulls the fingerprint card to compare for a confirmation. Many individuals can have the same sequence of print classifications but not be a match.)

Even if the requested agency does maintain such a system, the inquiring agency is much more likely to get a match if it has some idea as to the suspect's name because otherwise the receiving agency must search all the B of I files individually until a match is found or not. It can take weeks and even then, most replies are negative.

Personally, the only decedent Sheriff Harned expected to identify by fingerprint comparison with minimal effort was Mr. Elgin LaRue, most likely by the Cincinnati Police Department and/or the Hamilton County, Ohio Sheriff's Office. Even that was far from certain; but, if LaRue were positively identified maybe some of the other decedents would be also, especially if the Cincinnati authorities kept a list of known criminal associates for everyone they arrested.

This is information Sheriff Harned did not share with anybody, especially a news reporter. Ditto with respect to his staff of two, neither of whom were regarded as bright candles. Solving crimes usually means keeping a tight lid on proprietary information, otherwise known as tips, leads, clues, affidavits, statements, confessions, direct evidence, or even circumstantial evidence, etc., so that it does not work its way back to the perpetrators prematurely. Would you show your poker hand to the other players before all the bets were in and it was time to fish or cut bait? That basic concept was beyond the grasp of his loyal, helpful, gullible, well-intentioned, good-hearted deputies.

Sheriff Harned did tell Cub Reporter Quigley that he would release the names of each decedent as they became known. Finally, he said he did not have any suspects at this time and that he would wait to see what the commonwealth's special investigators planned to do before he made any further comments.

Oh Lordy! Gerard was concerned that the Ashland paper was getting too close to the truth. He hoped the commonwealth investigators would chase their tails trying to locate this mythical local moonshine empire, that is assuming they were intelligent enough to separate fact from the fanciful fiction that sells newspapers.

At 1:10, Sheriff Moses Harned, his dimwit son-in-law, Deputy Sheriff Bevis Bottoms, and Louisa Mayor Rupert W. Roe, Jr. strolled to the train station. Gerard reckoned that the absence of the geriatric Deputy Sheriff Dwayne Turley suggested that he was 'holding down the fort' at the jail. Gerard concluded that these three public servants constituted the official welcoming party for the governor's cadre of special investigators.

Gerard pondered the notable absences of Judge Durrell Durham, the highest-ranking elected official in Lawrence County (who was also the county executive by virtue of his position as judge), and of Commonwealth Attorney Angus Livingood (the county prosecutor). Did this mean the governor's men were unwelcome? Wouldn't that be something? Gerard had assumed the top two Lawrence County officials would be at the train station as a sign of respect for the governor, Republican or otherwise.

He came up with four possibilities: (1) emissaries from the highly unpopular, meddlesome Governor Morrow didn't merit their presence no matter how high-ranking the emissaries were, nor how much the governor valued their mission; (2) the elected leadership of Lawrence County had no intention of assisting the governor's men in rooting around in the lives of their constituents, whether they be moonshiners, bootleggers, and/or killers of out-of-state gangsters; (3) urgent county business dictated that both leading officials be elsewhere; or (4) all of the above.

Gerard hoped it was 1, 2, or 4. Anything except 3 by itself. That would just be lame.

At 1:20 on the dot, The Bluegrass Zephyr pulled into the station belching black smoke. Six men of the fourteen who disembarked joined together before identifying and walking over to their welcoming committee. They were led by an extremely tall, distinguished spokesman. Gerard noted the appearances and characteristics of each of these six men. His liberty might one day depend upon spotting them before they spotted him. He watched while they had a confabulation with the sheriff. Then Gerard got lucky.

The junior member of the group was a young lad, probably less than the age of majority. He appeared to be simple but perhaps not. Maybe he was just naive and eager to please his superiors. He appeared awfully young to be a special investigator. The leader dispatched him back to the stock car on the train to collect their horses. Deputy Bottoms was dispatched by Sheriff Harned to assist. Requisite pleasantries exchanged, Mayor Roe faded away in the direction of the courthouse, his goodwill mission being consummated. The sheriff took the other five strangers to the Dixie House Hotel to check in. Gerard wisely decided to follow the horses instead.

Deputy Bottoms lead the young man and the horses to Spellman's Livery Stable. Five minutes later, Deputy Bottoms made his exit. Once he was an afterthought, Gerard sauntered in, pretending to check on Jerome and Mabel.

Homer Spellman walked over to see if his old friend needed any help. Gerard shook his head 'no' and whispered, "Give me a few minutes. I need to talk to this kid alone." Homer winked and went back to mucking a stall.

Gerard left his draft horses and walked over to the stall where the kid was brushing a big bay with four white stockings. The other five state mounts, not nearly as handsome, including one brown mule, were in nearby stalls.

Gerard exclaimed, "Say, young feller, that's a mighty fine-lookin' stud you got there! Any of them otherns or that mule yourn? Reason I ask is, I just saw you lead 'em all over here and I thought my gosh, that's a passel of horseflesh for one man to shepherd all by hisself on a train."

"Call me Buster. My name is a Buster G. Black. Nope. They ain't none of 'em mine. This'n here belongs to my boss, Major Jubal Bohannan. He's famous. Maybe you heared of him."

"Who's famous - the horse or Major Bohannan?"

Buster erupted into a guffaw. "That's a good one! Not the horse! Major Bohannan! He's famous! Maybe you seen him when we got off the train. He's the tall feller. Six-and-a-half feet to be exact. They calls him Big Six on accounta he's so tall. He hails from Paducah. Surely you heared of him. He was a captain in charge of a cavalry troop durin' the Great War. He's a bonafide war hero. Kilt a lot of krauts. Got the Medal of Honor. He's the onliest livin' Kentuckian to have that medal. Now he's a major in the National Guard at headquarters in Frankfort. That's where I work. I enlisted. I'm a private. It's my job to do whatever the major needs."

"Golly! That sounds like a lot of responsibility for a private.

Pardon me for sayin' so, but you don't look old enough to be a soldier."

"I am, though. I'm sixteen. I joined up on my birthday six months ago. My pappy signed for me. It's steady work and we need the pay. Besides, I love my job. Someday I'll be like Major Bohannan."

"Tell me some more about your boss. Seems like maybe I heared something about a soldier from Kentucky getting that medal a couple of year ago."

"Okay. Maybe this will help recollect your memory. The krauts invented some newfangled cannon that could shoot farther than anything we had. They could hide it behind a hill and bombard a target without even being able to see it. Like th'owin' a dirt clod over a house and hittin' somebody on the other side ever' time without ever missin' but too far away for the other guy to th'ow one back, but if'n he did, he couldn't see where to th'ow it. Can you imagine that?"

"I can."

"Okay. So, the krauts was killin' our boys with these new cannons but we couldn't do anything about it. Finally, a two-star general asked for volunteers to go on a secret mission to destroy those cannons. Some even said it was a suicide mission. Major Bohannan was a captain back then. He volunteered and so did eight other men. What they done was flank the krauts on the right past most of their sentries in the middle of the night. Then they cut deep into enemy territory. They went on horseback as far as they could. They had to hide in a shelled farmhouse afore it got light.

"They holed up until the next night. By then those new kraut cannons had started firin' at our lines again so our boys knowed exactly where they was. They sneaked up on 'em from behind whilst they was sleepin' and kilt ever'one of the cannoneers by slicin' their throats with bayonets so as not to make any noise and wake up other kraut soldiers nearby.

"They was four of these great big cannons. Big, long barrels. They never seen nothin' like 'em afore. Next thing they done was break the sightin' apparatus so they couldn't be used again. I ain't never seen a sightin' apparatus but I know it's something important. Then they put explosives down in the cannon barrels and blowed 'em all up at the same time.

"Kaboom! This woke up ever' kraut within ten miles and they commenced to come a runnin' for our boys. They run all night, stoppin' ever' now and again to shoot some of the krauts to slow 'em down. All our guys was kilt except for Major Bohannan and one other feller, Sergeant Nettles, but he was wounded real bad and Major Bohannan had to carry him the rest of the way on his back but he died anyway a few days later in the hospital. That's how brave Major Bohannan is. That's why they give him the Medal of Honor."

"I do remember that story but I didn't remember the name. Major Bohannan is the bravest man I ever heared of. By the way, what's the National Guard doing here all the way from Frankfort?"

"Oh, we ain't all in the National Guard. Just the major and me. But that ain't the major's onliest job. He's the feller in charge of the governor's bodyguards. Four guys report to him. The governor really trusts him. He sent us here on account of the moonshine war where all them fellers got kilt. Told Major Bohannan to pick any five guys he wanted to go with him. Major Bohannan picked me afore anyone else because he trusts me to take care of the horses. I always been good with horses. Governor Morrow swore us all in as special investigators on Thursday. It's a big honor. My pappy says so."

"My gosh! That's an important job. Who else did he pick besides you?"

"Did you see us all standing around at the train depot?"

"Sure did."

"Well, if you saw a short, heavyset feller in a green plaid suit and a brown derby hat and white spats, he's our number two. That's Mr. C.K. Whipple. He's Governor Morrow's son-in-law. He graduated from Yale College. He was a second lieutenant in the Great War in the Quartermasters. They's the ones in charge of supplies and transportation. His job on this trip is mostly to keep track of the money and write the reports and get us whatever we need."

"Like what?"

"Oh, anything. He lined up the horses, made sure everyone had a reliable gun and enough ammo. He got us hotel rooms, paid for the train tickets, makes sure we all get paid on time, stuff like that. We couldn't do our job without him greasin' the skids. Besides, who's gonna argue with the governor's son-in-law?"

"Did he get ever'one a gun?"

"No. Only if'n they didn't have one or they needed a better one. Whatever kind you like - rifle, pistol, or shotgun, assuming it's in inventory or don't cost too much. Example. I didn't have no gun. I picked me out a Model 12 Winchester pump shotgun. It's a twelve-gauge. Kicks like the dickens but I'm used to it now. Some of our boys carried them in the trenches during the Great War. It's Army surplus but they said they'll let me buy it for five bucks. They also give me a box of 25 double-aught buck shells. I asked for two but Mr. Whipple said it would be a waste of money because Major Bohannan probably wouldn't let me ride with 'em on the missions. We'll see about that! I bet I get out more'n he does! He's a bean counter, not a fightin' man!"

"Mr. Whipple get him a gun, too?"

"Yep. He picked out a Springfield .30-06 but heaven only knows why. Maybe he needs it for shootin' varmints back home. All I know is, that's a lot of rifle for a short chubby guy. It's Army surplus, too. I'm pretty sure he won't need it here. Mostly he'll stay back wherever we set up shop, which I think will be the sheriff's office. He definitely ain't what you call a foot soldier but he's the best we got for doin' anything else."

"What about the others? Anyone else need a gun?"

"Well, Major Bohannan already had a government model .45. He wears it in a holster on his side every day. I think it's the same one he carried in the war. The onliest thing he ordered was eight extra magazines and he got 'em. He only had two magazines afore this. He also wanted two hundred rounds of ammo. He got all that too but he's the boss and can have any darn thing he wants. Nobody else got that much ammo.

"Then there's Beau Greathouse. He already had two Colt Peacemakers. All Mr. Whipple did was buy him ammo. He bought him two boxes of fifty rounds each."

"Who's Beau Greathouse?"

"His given name is Beauregard Greathouse. He was a Pinkerton detective most of his life. He's the old guy. Has thick white hair and a handlebar mustache. He was the one dressed like Wyatt Earp with a wide-brim, black Stetson and a coat that's longer than most fellers wear today. He's from Oklahoma originally but he moved to Kentucky from Chicago. Anyone'd be

a fool to cross him. He's our best shot. Heck! He's the best shot
anywhere he goes. He's put a lot of bandits six feet under. That's
why Major Bohannan selected him."

"Who else you all got?"

"Arthur T. Jackson. He's the little guy what dresses like a
dandy. Wears a bright red vest and a gold pocket watch and
chain. He carries a nickel-plated Smith & Western .32 caliber
revolver in a shoulder holster. He already had it. Mr. Whipple
bought him one box of ca'tridges. He was a hotel detective in San
Francisco and before that a railroad dick in Louisville for the
L&N. They say he's a whiz bang investigator. I don't know if'n
he is, 'cause I just met him on this trip. I do know he requested a
gaited horse and Mr. Whipple got it for him. I ain't sure how to
figger that since Mr. Whipple don't seem to cotton to him.

"Then our last guy is Clayton E. Simpson. You might not 'ave
noticed him. He's the kind of feller nobody notices in a crowd.
He's got real pale skin and red hair. He's the one dressed in a
brown suit, no vest, olive green tie, brown fedora with a floppy
brim and brown hightop shoes. He was a deputy sheriff in El
Paso, Texas, for about ten years. Then he quit and joined the
Army. Rode with General Blackjack Pershing when they was
chasin' Pancho Villa and the Mexican Army, who was really just
bandits. Clayton got hisself shot in the shoulder in a firefight with
those darn Mexican bandits down there. Got discharged from the
Army in 1917 after his serve-out afore they started draftin' for the
Great War but he already done his time. He carries a .38 Smith &
Western, double-action revolver in a cross-draw holster on his
belt. Mr. Whipple got him two boxes of bullets because he likes
him better than Arthur, who can be a disagreeable cuss. He's the
feller who requested that brown mule. Also, he's the only one of

us that has ever been a sworn lawman."

"That's all of you special investigators?"

"Yep."

"How are six men supposed to stop a moonshine war?"

"Beats me. They ain't said. Major Bohannan is supposed to meet with the sheriff and find out who he thinks done all the killin'. Then I guess we'll go get 'em and put 'em in jail."

"Did you all get sworn in with full police powers?"

"What's that?"

"Did they say you could arrest people?"

"Nope, but they didn't say we couldn't."

"Do you know what the plans are for tomorrow?"

"Not yet, but I s'pose Major Bohannan will tell us at supper. We meet at the hotel lobby at six o'clock. Mr. Whipple pays for all our meals."

"Well good luck to you then. I'll probably still be in town tomorrow, at least in the mornin'. Maybe I'll see you afore one of us leaves."

"That would be nice. Good luck to you, too. Good day."

Chapter 16
The Intelligence Takes a Turn for the Worse

Gerard walked back to Jerome's stall and waited for Homer to come over. When he did, Gerard whispered, "Do you know anyone in the courthouse who might pass along a tip on the hush-hush?"

"I think so. What do you want to know?"

"Well, that kid I was talkin' to is one of the six special investigators. I'm tryin' to find out if'n they have arrest powers. The kid doesn't know. I was wonderin' if'n they had to be swore in by Judge Durham so's to have arrest powers in Lawrence County, or if'n they was swore in at Frankfort as lawmen with arrest powers all over the state. If'n so, I never heared of such a thing."

"Me neither. That's a good question. My nephew, Henry Hobgood, works in the county clerk's office. Basically, all he does is file legal documents but he hears ever'thing that goes on in the courthouse. I'll see what he knows."

"Thanks. Here's the deal. If'n they do have arrest powers, they can go wherever they want and lock up whoever they want and we might not hear about it until they show up unannounced. But if'n they can't, they'll have to take the sheriff or one of his deputies with 'em to make the arrest. That means we got a shot at bein' tipped off. See the importance?"

"Yep. It could make the difference betwixt freedom and jail or worser. I'll let you know what I find out later today."

"Thanks."

Gerard didn't have anything left to do while he was waiting so he stopped by Miss Maybelle's Cafe for an early supper. No matter. It was because he never got around to eating lunch. The first thing he noticed was the fellow that nobody notices. Mr. Clayton E. Simpson was sitting by himself, polishing off a slice of apple pie and sipping on a cup of coffee. He was reading a copy of the *Ashland Telegraph*. He had the look of a competent, thoughtful lawman - not kind you'd wanna mess with.

Gerard was confused. At least three of these special investigators were top-notch men. The other three might be also. They were the antithesis of the Cincinnati gangsters. He did not want to go to war with them, even if they were misguided regarding their assigned mission to eradicate moonshining from Lawrence County. Gerard never even really considered that their primary mission was to bring the gangster killers to justice.

For goodness sakes! What kind of misguided idiot could possibly believe there was something wrong with slaying all those vile predators after all they done and was tryin' to do? They weren't human beings! They were dangerous animals!

Then he thought. Maybe the idiots were the same type of fools who blamed Wyatt Earp for killing the so-called cowboys who were in reality, rustlers, thieves, armed robbers, and cold-blooded murderers. Gerard said a silent prayer. He prayed that the special investigators would leave him alone so he could leave them alone. Same thing for all the other citizens who stood up with him and Jack and lopped the heads off those nine pit vipers.

It was about seven o'clock when Homer stopped by the stable to relay what he learned. Judge Durham did not swear in the special investigators as temporary peace officers in Lawrence

County. He was outraged that Governor Morrow even suggested it. The mere suggestion, which in actuality was more of a strong-arm demand than a request, implied that Sheriff Harned and his deputies were incompetent or dishonest or both. Judge Durham took that as a personal affront.

Judge Durham decreed that, if the investigators need a search warrant or an arrest warrant, they must bring their affidavit to the court for his consideration. Commonwealth Attorney Livingood agreed to assist in drafting affidavits with them if they need legal advice. If the investigators' paperwork is in order, the judge will take Major Bohannan's oath, witness his signature, sign his own name, place his seal on the document, and give it to Sheriff Harned, who will be present as the peace officer when they execute it. Judge Durham stated emphatically, one last time before bidding Major Bohannan adieu, that the investigators do not have authority to make an arrest based upon probable cause in Lawrence County.

Gerard let out a sigh of relief before uttering his silent gratitude to God. The only thing left for him to do now, was to try to wheedle more information from Buster, particularly about their plans, assuming he could get him alone.

Since Gerard was sleeping in the stable, he was perfectly situated to accidentally bump into Buster when he came in to groom the horses in the morning.

Buster showed up a little after six. He was all alone. Gerard made sure that Buster saw him harnessing his horses. Gerard wanted to be on the road as soon as he milked Buster for all the information he would share.

"Hey, there, Buster! You're bright and early this mornin'."

"Yep. Major Bohannan's got me on a short leash today. He

done told me to have all the animals but one ready to ride by seven o'clock. We got a lot of miles to cover. Guess who ain't included in the trip today."

"Well, I know the Major couldn't get along without you. You're way too valuable. I'm guessin' Mr. C.K. Whipple is stayin' behind today."

"You got it! Told ya so, didn't I? I oiled and loaded my shotgun last night after I found out."

"Where y'all goin'."

"That I don't know. What I do know is this. There's a powerful holy roller in the Baptist church here who was a fraternity brother with Governor Morrow at Transylvania College. I don't know who he is but he really hates the demon alcohol. He give the governor a list of moonshiners that he says could've been involved in the massacre. So, beginnin' today, we're goin' to start payin' those boys a visit. Major says we don't need no warrant to look for a still so long as we stay out of the curtilage. Don't matter what the property owner says. Chief Justice John D. Carroll of the Kentucky Supreme Court, hisself, says so and he give the major a written order to show to anyone who questions it."

"You know what a curtilage is?"

"Well, I know it means the house and the barn and the yard. Not sure about anything else but Major Bohannan will be there to tell us if we have a question."

"My gosh! What if the owner says you're trespassin' and gotta leave?"

"That's not the way Judge Carroll sees it nor the way Major Bohannan sees it. They say it ain't trespassin'. We won't trespass in the curtilage but we'll check the rest of the farm anyway."

"Is that the way you see it?"

"No, but I ain't as smart as they are. It don't matter how I see it."

"Buster, this could turn into one bloody gunfight after another. You sure you all are ready for that?"

"Well, if'n we're outnumbered, we'll leave and the major will call in the National Guard. Then we'll come back. If'n they resist we'll take 'em by force."

"Do you hear what you're sayin'? Are you prepared to kill Kentuckians because the governor don't like alcohol? If'n you try to do this, they'll send you all home in caskets on the same train what brung you here."

"Maybe so. Nevertheless, that's our orders. I'll do what the major tells me to do, even if'n it gets me killed."

"Is Sheriff Harned goin' with you all?"

"Nope. He said he wasn't bein' no party to this. I get it. He lives here. He could never get elected again if'n he done this. That's why the governor sent us."

"Know who any of the so-called suspects are?"

"Nope. Major didn't say. He said he routed us so we don't have to plow the same ground twicet. May only get to one farm a day. He did say they was some automobiles blowed up down in the southern part of the county. The holy roller thinks it was part of the massacre. I know we're goin' to check that out but it won't be for a few days yet. That's all he said.

"Look, I hate to be rude but I gotta get goin' or the major will get after me. Maybe we'll meet again someday. If'n I get killed, come to my funeral, okay?"

"Don't even joke about that, Buster. You all are fixin' to trample on ever'one's God-given Constitutional rights. They won't stand for it. You might not know it, but you're about to grab the tiger by the tail. I'll tell you what I will do. I'll say a prayer for you. That's about all I can promise."

"I never asked your name, mister, but I ain't jokin'. All this here is bigger than me. I'm just a private. I don't think this sounds right but I gotta do what the major tells me. Best luck to you. I hope you ain't one of the fellers on the list."

"My name is Gerard Silas Twyman. I hope I ain't on your list neither, nor none of my neighbors, nor my kin, nor my friends. If'n any of us are, then understand that I gotta do what my conscience tells me. My family's fought for our God-given rights since we first come over from the old country in the 1700's. Some of 'em was kilt fightin' for freedom and liberty. That includes fightin' Yankees, too. A man never knows what he's made of until him or his family or his rights are threatened. They say 'a coward dies a thousand deaths. A hero only dies oncet.'"

"Right you are. I need to remember that."

"Take care, Buster."

"You, too, Mr. Twyman."

Chapter 17:
Gerard Briefs Jack

Gerard made a beeline for Rabbit Bluff. He didn't tarry along the way. He arrived at dusk. Jack was unwinding on the verandah with his pipe and a jug of elixir. The cicadas were chirping and the lightning bugs were twinkling like miniature fairies.

Jack helped Gerard stow the canvas tent and bivouac supplies in the barn near his cot. They tended to the horses' needs, after which Gerard gobbled up the rest of the cornbread, country ham, black-eyed peas, and applesauce left over from Jack's supper. Then they plopped down in the two cedar rockers on the verandah that Gerard recently acquired from Grady Gillespie in return for a half-dozen quarts of hundred-proof happy juice.

Jack watched Gerard pour himself a full cup of elixir so he did likewise. This was an obvious sign that the news was anything but good. Jack and Gerard lit up, smoking and sipping for about fifteen minutes, neither having uttered a word. Jack held his peace and concentrated on keeping his pipe lit.

It must have been shortly before Jack's fortieth birthday when Gerard finally began to recount everything he saw, heard, and did in town. They had both consumed a second cup of elixir by the time he concluded. Jack did not interrupt. He had a tight knot in his stomach. They filled their pipes with more tobacco and poured a third cup of elixir.

Finally, Jack asked, "Do you know who the self-righteous rat is?"

"No, but I bet Mr. Mac will know. We'll go over and see him first thing in the mornin'. I also don't know who's on the list of suspects but I'm pretty sure I'm on it and you prob'ly are too if'n the snake-in-the-grass knows you've come back home. That's why you gotta keep your head down. We'd be in a terrible fix if'n we was both kilt or hauled off to the calaboose. You and me gotta write our wills tomorrow morning naming each other as beneficiary. We'll get Mr. Mac to witness and hold 'em for us."

"You gonna alert the guys who was with us?"

"You're dern right I am. Me and Mr. Mac will do that tomorrow. I hope it won't be too late for any of 'em. Whilst we're doin' that, I want you to tidy up things around here. Find yourself a rabbit hole on Mr. Mac's property to set up. It can't be too far from Rabbit Bluff, else it will take us too long to render aid to each other.

"Jack, I ain't lettin' no commonwealth investigators creep all over my property against my wishes without no warrant signed by Judge Durham just because some high muckety-muck in Frankfort said it's legal. That's hogwash! This is still America! I may not be no war veteran like you but I'm still a true-blue patriot to the red, white, and blue and I ain't knucklin' under to no governor-appointed tyrant whether he has the Medal of Honor or not. You with me on that? You believe this is cause enough to die for? If'n not, let me know now."

"I do, Cousin. That gives me an idea. When you're out runnin' around like Paul Revere tomorrow shoutin' 'the British are comin'! The British are comin'!' stop by Woodrow Falstaff's and buy us a flag. You got a pole out in the barn we can hang it on. Heck, I'll put it up tomorrow while you're gone. That way if we get kilt and all sorts of folks are nosing around here, reporters, lawmen, neighbors, and God knows how many busybodies, maybe one of 'em will snap to it that we're the good guys defending our Constitutional rights. It would pain me almost as bad to be thought of as a traitor, as it would to be thought of as a coward."

"Jack, I don't have to. I already got a flag in my chest. Of course this'n only has 47 stars. My pappy bought it after they made the Territory of New Mexico a state. Heck, if he'd a waited just a couple more months, he coulda got one with 48 stars when they added Arizona."

"It'll do just fine. I doubt anyone will take the time to count all the stars. How many days you think we got?"

"Maybe three or four and today counts as number one. I know for sure that Major Bohannan is focused on those blowed up cars."

"What if we move 'em somewhere else?"

"Like where?"

"I don't know. You tell me."

"Hmm. I got it! You remember Old Man Ellis?"

"June Bug Ellis? The old Negro who was a freed slave? Had a few acres on the cutback behind Mr. Mac's?"

"That's him! He passed away a year or so ago. He has five or six kids. He didn't have no will. The kids are still fightin' over who gets what. Anyway, his place is deserted. It's overrun with weeds and briars and such. He has an old barn that's about to collapse. If'n we could take the vehicles out in pieces, we could put 'em in his barn. Of course, Walter Limehouse told me some time back that he was over there and the property is crawlin' with copperheads, so be careful. Anyway, what about you hitchin' up the horses tomorrow and seein' if'n this would even be possible. If'n it is, I can help you on Thursday. I got a pulley in the barn as well as axes and a sledge hammer. Whaddaya think?"

"If it's doable, I'll get a head start on it tomorrow. You think the investigators will make it out here by Friday?"

"I don't know. I hope not. Tell you what. Whether we can move them machines or not, take the license plates off of 'em and bury 'em somewhere in the woods far away from where I blowed 'em up. That should make it harder for them to determine ownership."

"Will do. I'm all worn out. I'm hitting the rack. See you in the morning."

"Good night, Cousin."

Chapter 18:
Preparing for the Inevitable Confrontation

Wednesday was a busy day. Gerard and Jack were standing outside Mr. Mac's front door by seven o'clock. He was thrilled to see them. He invited them in for coffee.

First things first. The boys brought him their handwritten wills. They signed and dated them in his presence. Then he signed them as their witness. He placed them in a metal box which he stored in a sea chest at the end of his bed.

Next, Gerard reiterated everything he told to Jack the night before. When he was through, Mr. Mac said, "The informant is Mervin Bledsoe. His daddy was Everett A. Bledsoe, who was the orneriest cuss in Boyd County back in the day. He owned the lion's share of Ashland Oil afore he lost it all drinkin' and gamblin' and womanizin'. When Mervin went off to Transylvania College, his daddy was one of the richest men in Eastern Kentucky. When he come back home after graduation, his family was broke and livin' in disgrace.

"Seems like old Everett had embezzled thousands of dollars from the company. He was under indictment and facin' twenty years at hard labor but he never did go to trial. One night a few days afore it was scheduled to begin, old Everett got hisself riproarin' drunk and fell down the stairs and broke his neck at Celeste Harper's fancy cathouse. He was never convicted so in the eyes of the law he died innocent. I heared he owed Celeste a chunk of change, too. Prob'ly the best outcome for old Everett under the circumstances. At least he got his ashes hauled afore he died. I pray to God I'm that lucky.

"Anyway, Mervin became a very bitter, spoilt, young man. He got a job with the Pearson Coal Mine Company in their business office. He done real well, too. He married the owner's second oldest daughter - he had five but this'n was the homeliest one - and that's all it took. Mervin was rollin' in clover all over again, literally and figuratively with his plump, and not too bright but very rich new bride, Esther. He joined the First Self-Righteous Church in Fallsburg, Kentucky, not too far from where we ambushed those mobsters and . . ."

Gerard interrupted, "Mr. Mac, I ain't never heared of no such sect of a church."

"Well, that's prob'ly 'cause that's what I named it. It's really a hardshell Baptist denomination, but once Mervin made deacon and since he had more money than the whole congregation added together, he got to have the most say in how the church operates and what they do. Mervin's money allows him to use his self-righteousness as a whip whenever he feels like torturing those poor souls. It makes him feel important.

"But you know what? While it's true Mervin don't drink, he does fornicate regularly with Esther's little sister, Eunice, who is real easy on the eyes. She's ten years younger than Esther, and what you would call pulchritudinous. Her hubby, Darren Trahan, died of pneumonia a couple of years back. Ever' Thursday betwixt noon and two when Esther is at her quilting circle, old Mervin goes over to Eunice's to fix her plumbing."

"What? You mean . . . ?"

"Oh yes, indeed. He's laid a lot of pipe in her house over the past couple of years but apparently Eunice still needs weekly maintenance."

"How do you know?"

"My young friend, I am well-acquainted with more than a few widows in Lawrence County who appreciate discreet servicing of their plumbing needs oncet or twicet a month, but by appointment only. I ain't the onliest plumber either, and that's how I'm gonna rain pee on Mervin's parade for siccin' these state dogs on us."

"How you gonna do that?"

"I'm gonna send Mervin a telegram to his home which says, "What if a deacon was exposed for having an illicit affair with a family member? Would the church ex-communicate him? Would he lose his family and his job? Just wondering. Signed, The All-knowing Eyeball."

"Are you gonna expose him?"

"Oh heck no! I don't want to embarrass Eunice. I just want to make Mervin sweat. Have some sleepless nights. Make him see the error of his ways. Take all the starch outta him. He'll be sweatin' about who all knows his secret. It might cause him performance issues. That'll be punishment enough unless some of our friends or us gets wracked up by the governor's posse. If'n that happens, then I'll have to come up with a worser punishment."

"Couldn't he track the message to the telegraph operator and then back to you?"

"Very unlikely. Old Oswald Jenkins down at Western Union is an old friend of mine. He'll get a chuckle out of this but I'll slip him a few bucks extra to seal the deal. However, if'n he does, so what? Mervin's a cowardly yella cur dog. Ain't nothin' he can do to me. I don't owe a penny to a soul and I ain't afeared of him. I'll punch his ticket if'n he thinks otherwise.

"Boys, we gotta get us a move on. Gerard, you go pay a visit to your old buddies, and I'll go see mine. Jack, you move as much of those blowed up machines as you can. Try not to get seen. Use a tarp when you're travelin'. Meet back here tonight and I'll fix us some beef stew. You all bring the libation. We'll compare notes. If'n all is well, I'll hitch up a team and we'll finish the disappearin' act together tomorrow."

"You got it. See ya about sundown."

For Jack, this turned into a long, difficult day. His easiest task was removing the license plates from the hulks and burying them in a remote location. He did that first thing since it was critical.

Next, he piled parts which had blown off the automobiles into the wagon. When it was full, he drove it to June Bug's dilapidated barn and threw them all the way in the back. It was a half-mile each way. Easy-peasy. He made three trips.

The next chore and the hardest yet, was removing parts from the hulks and putting them in the wagon. Doors, fenders, hoods, spare wheel rims, and so forth. Some were easy. Some were not. Six trips.

It was getting late. He managed to remove the Maxwell engine from its chassis. He used the pulley to place it in the wagon. He dumped it in the barn. His last trip.

That concluded his backbreaking work for the day. Tomorrow would be much more difficult, but with three of them working and two wagons, they should be able to finish the job.

Jack was filthy, covered with soot and grease. On the way home he stopped at the creek and doused himself clothes and all in the creek. Too bad he didn't have any soap. Not a great cleansing but it beat getting a sharp stick in the eye.

He got home before Gerard so he washed himself and his

clothes with hot soapy water in the tub. He put on his other set of farm clothes which were newer and nicer and clean. He hung his wet clothes up to dry. He would wear them again tomorrow. Save his clean clothes for jobs which don't involve burnt, carbon-covered dirt.

Gerard was in a tizzy when he returned. He saddled Tulip for Jack before he even entered the cabin. He retrieved a gallon jug of elixir from their near stash. He prodded Jack to get the lead out. It was nearly eight o'clock by the time they arrived at Mr. Mac's.

Their 'stomachs were touching their backbones.' They had all fasted since breakfast. They devoured the stew in slurpy silence like ravenous wolves, 'licking the platter clean' in a manner of speaking. Not a morsel left. Then they filled their pipes and cups and set about to jawboning.

Chapter 19:
Assessing the Situation

Mr. Mac spoke first. He had met with Lige Bostick, Adrian Pullman, and Rufus Claiborne. All of them knew about the governor's investigators. They also heard that Judge Durham and Sheriff Harned were not cooperating with them. In fact, the governor's boys had riled up Judge Durham to the extent that either Judge Durham might get removed from office by the governor (if he has the power and right now no one knows for sure), or Major Bohannan and possibly some of his men might get charged criminally.

Gerard exclaimed, "What?"

"Yep. Rufus has a cousin who lives up near Buchanan. Apparently, the major decided to start at the north end and work his way south. On Tuesday the posse raided the farm of some unfortunate soul named Lucius McGillicuddy. He's a dirt-poor pig farmer on fourteen acres with a wife and eight kids. They's barely eking out a livin'. I reckon he was on Mervin's list of suspects. They ain't neighbors but they live in the same neck of the woods.

"Anyway, poor old Lucius has a one-barrel rig. Him and his oldest boy was runnin' off a batch when the posse sneaked up on 'em. They caught Lucius afore he knew what hit him but his boy, Phineas, was alert and grabbed the shotgun. It weren't nothin' but a single-shot sixteen-gauge but the minute he laid hands on it, one of the investigators, a little weasel with a hideout gun shot him in the leg and he dern near bled to death.

"They carried him to Doc Dollinger's office in Louisa. Then they hauled old Lucius afore Judge Durham and said they wanted to swear out a warrant on him for distillin' untax-paid liquor and another warrant on his boy for assaultin' the weasel who shot him."

Gerard exclaimed, "What gall!"

Mr. Mac continued, "Well, Judge Durham blowed a gasket. You hear me? He pointed at Lucius and screamed, 'He look like a threat to society to you? Look at him? He ain't eaten a full meal in months! I know him and his family! They ain't never hurt a soul! Plus, you shot his fourteen-year-old son when he realized he was bein' sneaked up on by armed men he never saw afore and all while he was standin' peaceably on his own daddy's land! Did you identify yourselves as lawmen? No, because you ain't! You had no business bein' there! I can assure you neither this man nor his boy had anythin' to do with killin' those gangsters! Major, I warned you about this! You have grossly overstepped!'

"He told 'em to stand down while he decided if'n he was goin' to instruct the commonwealth attorney to have the sheriff file charges against 'em. He said they better not leave town if'n they knowed what was good for 'em. Then he told Lucius to stay put and he th'owed the major and his men out of his courtroom."

Jack exclaimed, "Holy cow!"

Gerard said, "I guarantee the shooter is the feller named Arthur T. Jackson. I seen him when he got off'n the train.

"I hadn't heared none of this 'til now. Well, I spoke with Bloody Gene Whalen, Herschel Wilson, and T. Rex Tapp. So far, the investigators haven't bothered Wilson or Whalen. However, they stopped by T. Rex's place, too. This must've been afore they went to McGillicuddy's. T. Rex hails from a big clan and he was ready and waitin' for 'em. They rode up and stopped just short of the picket fence surroundin' his yard. They never dismounted. The reason was, there must've been eight or nine of T. Rex's kinfolk standin' in the yard with him. They was all armed to the teeth. T. Rex was holdin' that ten-gauge lever-action of his.

"The major said he had reliable information that T. Rex was operatin' a still. T. Rex said 'horse feathers' and told the major to quit wastin' his time. He said they was trespassin' and to get off'n his property - all 857 acres of it.

"The major said he had the lawful authority to search it for a still. T. Rex said 'We'll see about that' and told him if'n they tried, it would be at their own peril because on Tapp property they shoot trespassers. Said his fences was all posted with that warnin'.

"The major said, 'Fine,' he would be back with a platoon of national guardsmen within a week. Then T. Rex told him he better bring the whole dern comp'ny because that's how many it would take if'n he come back. He also said the ground would be soaked with the blood of bullies and tyrants and that none of 'em would return home in one piece. Then the major said, 'Another day,' and he and his men rode off."

Mr. Mac said, "Dern! The major's not goin' to back down and we don't know what the judge will decide. We can't sit idly by on our hands and wait for cooler heads to prevail or we'll get caught with our pants down. The major won't try Tapp again unless the governor sends him a troop of National Guard but he might well try you, especially if'n he wants to catch the jaybirds who blowed up them machines on my property."

"We gotta move those vehicles off'n my property tomorrow. If'n someone's tipped him to where they're at, he'll prob'ly do what Elgin LaRue did and come through thataway to search your property without even stoppin' by your cabin.

"Tell you what. Let's call it a night, boys. I'll meet you there in the mornin'. We know for the posse to get here on horseback from town while it's still daylight, they'd have to set out afore the cock crows. That pushes them showin' up here back to Friday at the earliest. We should be done afore dusk but to play it safe, come loaded for bear."

Thursday was a labor-intensive day but three of them working in concert made an enormous difference. They discovered it was easier to pull the chassis to the barn with a double team of draft horses than it was to dismantle everything, even though the rubber tires had been all burned off. They spent as much time covering their tracks as they did hauling off the automobile carcasses. They even made deep wagon track ruts to the road leading to Mr. Mac's house to further obfuscate matters.

After all that work, they realized that even if Major Bohannan's posse did find the vehicles, it wouldn't further his cause one whit. He would still need to identify the party/parties unknown who had detonated them and prove it, but who and where were the victims and/or the witnesses? As Winston Churchill said when he described the intentions of the Soviet Union pre-World War Two, "It was a riddle, wrapped in a mystery, inside an enigma."

Chapter 20:
Time Draws Closer

On Friday Jack collected his gear for bivouacking. He and Cousin Gerard and Mr. Mac had done all they could in preparation for an altercation. (Jack didn't want to call it a showdown since the adversaries were commonwealth-appointed agents. He prayed there would be no bloodshed.) He nodded at (like quiet, strong men do) and shook hands with Gerard, no words being necessary. He mounted the overloaded Tulip and headed to Old MacEwen's farm.

Jack selected a secluded spot near the bubbling limestone creek which was only fifty yards from the invisible boundary between Rabbit Bluff and Mr. Mac's. He dumped his stuff and hobbled Tulip downstream where she could drink water and feed on the shaded, tender, succulent, bright blue-green bluegrass.

He set up the two-man tent, dug a trench around it to carry off water in case it rained, collected stones for a fire ring, and gathered dry wood for fires. He even found a log big enough to sit on which he dragged next to his fire ring. He stowed all his gear neatly in the tent. When he was done, he stood back and looked at his camp with a critical eye. He was quite pleased with it. It was much better than his digs in France during the Great War except for the night he spent in a hotel.

Jack spent the afternoon traipsing through the woods, double-checking on the sanctity of the still site, hidden caves, tells, and in making a determination as to how long it would take him to get back to the cabin if he heard three, evenly-spaced pistol shots, which was their signal to come fast because all Hell's broken loose. He figured it would take thirty minutes on foot and a little less than half that on Tulip. Either way it would be way too late to be of assistance. They both inherently knew that but pretended otherwise.

Everything was quiet and serene. Jack watched Gerard weeding the garden for awhile and thought how bucolic it was at Rabbit Bluff.

That night he fixed himself some country ham, canned Lima beans, and canned pears for supper. He capped the night off with a campfire, elixir, and his pipe. So far, so good.

Saturday morning Jack checked the corked bottle in the crook of the hedge apple tree to see if he had a message from Gerard. He did not. He decided to keep a watch on the demolished vehicle site. He watched all afternoon. 'All quiet on the western front.' He walked back to his camp. He saddled Tulip and rode over to Mr. Mac's to see if he had any news.

Mr. Mac invited him to a supper of smoked sausage links dipped in brown mustard, fried potatoes, and cornbread with butter. Jack provided the untax-paid beverage.

Mr. Mac said he drove to town Friday night in his Model T and met a lady friend for supper at Bradbury's Beef Emporium. While they were dining, Major Bohannan and Mr. C.K. Whipple were seated at an adjacent table. They were quietly arguing about their lack of success. Mr. Mac could observe for himself that the plump son-in-law to Governor Morrow was a pompous, aggravating, sniveling toad. On the other hand, Major Bohannan was a stalwart adversary. It was obvious that even though the major was in charge, his second-in-command had all the political clout. This is what Mr. Mac overheard.

Governor Morrow wants scalps hanging on the wall now. Right away. He wants real Neanderthals, like the mountain clan leaders Anse Hatfield and Randolph McCoy of times long past, brought to justice. Those are the kind of men the yellow press in the big cities will chew up; not the pathetic, down-and-out sodbuster Bohannan dragged in and brought before Judge Durham. That pathetic soul is obviously too weak and scared to have been part of the crew who wiped out the gang from Cincinnati and everybody knows it.

For God's sake, it was all the governor could do to keep Art Jackson from going to jail for panick-shooting Lucius McGillicuddy's boy who isn't even old enough to shave yet! What is wrong with that man? You picked him! Your problem!

Not only that, Judge Durham has powerful friends in the legislature who vehemently oppose Prohibition and they're kicking up a dust storm. The governor is getting crucified in the public arena by all their followers over these lapses of judgment by Bohannan. As a result, there's no way the governor can send in the National Guard to search an influential taxpayer's property even if he is suspected of distilling untax-paid alcohol. The governor's hands are tied; however, if Bohannan hauls in a big fish then he might reconsider. In fact, that's exactly what it will take to salvage this whole operation.

The situation is dire. Things have changed. Whipple said if Major Bohannan can't capture someone who clearly was involved in the massacre of those mobsters by close of business Wednesday, with irrefutable evidence piled high on the table for the whole world to see, the governor's shutting everything down on that night. Poof! The stink will all be on Bohannan, not the governor!

The major listened patiently while Whipple railed on and on. When it was his turn, Bohannan uncorked. He laid out to Mr. Whipple 'how the cow ate the cabbage' in no uncertain terms. Whipple blanched with horror.

Bohannan said he was in charge of this expedition, not Whipple. If the governor has lost faith in him and decides to fire him, so be it. It won't be the end of the world. Something else will come up. Until then, Whipple better put a sock in it and get on board because Bohannan isn't the only one who's reputation is on the chopping block. When the governor's term is up, Whipple will be out of a job too, hoping to latch on with some other politician. People have long memories. Backstabbers get stabbed back. Whipple needs to bear that in mind.

Then Bohannan gave Whipple more bad news. The major said he had a fresh tip that a throwback to an earlier era, specifically a local crackpot by the name of Gerard Twyman, was one of the leaders of the group who ambushed the gangsters.

Bohannan said this tipster is better informed with more intimate knowledge of the local moonshine industry than the governor's college friend with his hit list of undesirables, said friend having very few, if any, influential friends here locally due to his sour and overbearing demeanor. Furthermore, his friend's father was an embezzler who stole thousands and thousands of dollars from the biggest and most prosperous company in Boyd County just in case Mr. Whipple didn't know. 'The apple doesn't fall far from the tree.'

Jack interrupted, and asked, "Where on Earth did Gerard's name come from?"

Mr. Mac said he didn't know, but it had to come from one of the men in the vigilante group, or perhaps a wife of one of them who gossiped to someone, who repeated it to someone else, who snitched to Major Bohannan, possibly for money or to get out of a jam. Mr. Mac said he spelled out all of this to Gerard just a little while ago and he couldn't think of anyone who would have knowingly fingered him or why.

Mr. Mac said for Jack to forget about the snitch for the time being because what he heard next was the important part.

Major Bohannan and the entire posse, to include Mr. C.K. Whipple, himself (greatly to his dismay), will bivouac somewhere close to Rabbit Bluff Sunday night. Mr. Mac doesn't know where. They plan to search Rabbit Bluff early Monday morning before knocking on Gerard's door. They hope to locate his still and with that proof, haul him in before Judge Durham. Gerard is the designated big fish, courtesy of this new informant.

Major Bohannan is fully committed to this raid being one hundred percent successful because now with the Wednesday deadline, he doesn't have time to search anyplace else if this is a bust. They'll every one of them return to Frankfort in disgrace. And that, more than anything else, is why Mr. Whipple will fully participate and get his hands dirty on this last venture despite all his whining and pleading. Major Bohannan said Mr. Whipple was acting like he didn't have a dog in this fight but he's wrong. They sink or swim together as a team.

Mr. Mac said Gerard wants Jack to set up on the gangster vehicle demolition site. The posse is bound to look there first. See where they go. If they get too close to the still, send the signal and beat feet back to the cabin.

Mr. Mac said, "We three will stand our ground and fight in the curtilage when the posse does show up. Gerard will have his flag flying Monday because this may well be our Alamo. Gerard said they probably won't be expecting a fight from a crackpot such as him, who doesn't have any help (except for the likes of you, if'n they know you're back from the Army.) They'll have numerical superiority and this will make them over-confident. That is our home court advantage."

Jack said he had checked the drop site earlier and Gerard hadn't left him a note.

Mr. Mac said if Jack checked now, he bet it would be there; but since the message has been passed, it was no longer necessary for him to check the drop site but to suit himself.

Jack agreed. He thanked Mr. Mac for the meal and the information. Then he rode back to his camp to get some rest and to collect his thoughts. Tomorrow he would do his final reconnaissance before selecting the best surveillance posts.

That night sitting before the campfire, sipping on a cup of elixir and smoking his pipe, Jack began to wonder.

He wondered how the posse would know where to search for Gerard's still since they had never been there before and nobody had drawn a map where "X" marks the spot.

Better yet, he wondered how they know where to begin looking for the gangster vehicle demolition site.

Then he wondered who ratted out Gerard.

He wondered if the traitor, Wilbur 'Dirty Bill' Conard, was still hiding in Fayette County.

He wondered if Dirty Bill was the rat. He certainly had an axe to grind with Gerard for shooting him in his posterior even though Gerard should have killed him. Six of the men who followed Dirty Bill onto Rabbit Bluff fought and were killed that day, yet for some reason Gerard had mercy and allowed Dirty Bill to live.

He wondered why.

He wondered if the posse was going to camp out at Dirty Bill's farm.

He wondered if he would see Dirty Bill Monday morning.

Finally, he wondered what he would do if he did.

Then he had an inspiration.

Chapter 21:
Asymmetric Warfare

Sunday morning was a beautiful spring day. The sky was cobalt blue with nary a cloud in sight. The weather was more than just pleasant. It was perfect. Low humidity. Temperature in the mid-sixties. Soft breeze rustling the leaves in the trees. Songbirds serenading. What more could you ask for?

Jack fixed a field breakfast consisting of coffee, country ham, common crackers, and canned peaches. Afterwards he saddled Tulip and reconnoitered Rabbit Bluff and the portion of Mr. Mac's property where the demolition site was located. Nothing had changed from the day before.

He rode to the cabin just to make sure everything was okay. Gerard was gone, most likely at church. Jack picked up a partial sack of oats for Tulip. He also found some carrots Gerard had pulled and cleaned. He fed one to Tulip. Gerard wouldn't care. He checked the drop site. Just like Mr. Mac had said, Gerard's note was there. Jack left a note that he was on board. Nothing more to do. He had time on his hands. He rode back to the camp.

He hobbled and curried Tulip by the creek. Then he walked away, out of her sight. He whispered, "I wish to be a red-tailed hawk for one hour. Afterwards, I want to return right here."

The next thing he knew, he was soaring over his camp. Outstanding! He was never certain if the changeling incantation would work exactly like he wanted it to, although to date, it always had. He was always afraid he would be stuck forever in a non-human format. Imagine living a thousand years like a field mouse. That's why he used this power sparingly. It would be foolish to tempt Fate. Who knows when the Apache god might change his mind and pull the rug out from under him.

Jack did not know where Dirty Bill's farm was located. He did know it was about two miles north of the demolition site, so using that as a starting point, he flew north. From a height of two hundred feet, he could see a broad expanse. The terrain was breathtaking.

He soared past a dozen or so farms, all surrounded by hardwood forests. Each one appeared to be too tidy and prosperous to be owned by the likes of Dirty Bill. Otherwise, why would he carry that monicker? It must encompass more than just his clothes or personal hygiene. Maybe it was his character. Jack just assumed it was a slur upon his whole being, including the way he lived.

Then in the distance, Jack spotted a derelict farm off to the east that might be it. The leaves on the cornstalks were yellow. They looked sickly like they needed water and some fertilizer. The buildings were run down. The grass (mostly weeds) in the curtilage was a foot tall and filled with debris - a broken upright piano, small, rusted farm implements, a wire cage of some sort, empty feed sacks, and so forth. Jack couldn't imagine any woman living in that hovel. He descended and perched on a dead limb high upon a sycamore tree. He would wait and see if any humans were about.

His patience paid off. Dirty Bill emerged from the barn. He walked with a slight limp. He was wearing bibs, a blue flannel shirt, and a floppy-brimmed black hat. His entire ensemble had seen better days. He was leading a mule outfitted with a McClellan saddle. (Probably the same mule Cousin Gerard ran off.) It was loaded with a rolled tarp. The saddlebags were bulging. He had two canteens. The saddle scabbard contained a long gun. Dirty Bill mounted and headed south down the dirt road. It was obvious he was headed to a bivouac, but where?

Jack was almost out of time. He whispered that he would like to have another hour as a hawk. His body felt strange. A shiver traveled up his spine. Then he was involuntarily launched way up into the air. He soared much higher than before. When he looked back down, Dirty Bill and his mule looked like an industrious black ant carrying a massive load - like a dead dung beetle. Jack figured he must be up at least four hundred feet above the ground. Dirty Bill would never notice him.

Dirty Bill rode probably two miles. He crossed over onto the property belonging to Nadine Compton, an elderly widow woman who lived with her son, Claude, and his wife and kids in Louisa. Claude owned the shoe repair shop but really, he fixed and sold just about anything made of leather. The Compton spread was not fenced in this area, nor was it posted, but it did back up to Mr. Mac's property and it was less than a mile to the demolition site. Jack doubted if the Compton's knew what Dirty Bill was up to.

Dirty Bill stopped and dismounted at a meadow bordered by the same creek which crosses Mr. Mac's property and Gerard's, as well as the twelve acres left to Jack as his inheritance at Rabbit Hollow. They called it the Blue Lick Creek whenever a person needed to be specific.

Jack watched while Dirty Bill took everything off his mount before hobbling it. So this must be the bivouac site. Jack watched long enough to be convinced and then he flew back towards his camp. He was almost there when poof! He found himself sitting up against the tree where he had started two hours earlier. He decided he must learn to keep better track of time. Of course, even though the mainspring had been replaced on his watch such that it now keeps time like the proverbial Swiss timepiece, red-tailed hawks don't carry watches. Neither do rabbits.

Jack thought about telling Gerard who the informant was and where the posse was camping. Then he realized Gerard would want to know how he found out. Jack couldn't tell him nor would he lie. He putzed around the camp the rest of the afternoon. He tried to take a nap but couldn't. It was a restless night. He was up well before the cock even considered crowing.

Jack rode Tulip towards the demolition site. He tethered her a couple of hundred yards away next to two wild crabapple trees. He didn't want her to be close enough to the other equines (when they arrived) that they might smell each other and start neighing or heehawing back and forth and thus alert the posse to his presence.

Jack walked to within thirty yards of the site on the near side closest to the still. He hunkered down in a shallow ravine and waited for the posse. He was wearing his gun belt but had left his shotgun in the saddle scabbard. He wanted to skedaddle as quickly as he could back to Tulip unencumbered if the situation called for it. His revolver would have to suffice for now.

The sun had been up for a couple of hours before Jack first heard them. They were riding single file. Dirty Bill was in the lead. Major Bohannan was next. Finally, they all arrived, surrounding and stopping around one of the burn circles.

Mr. Whipple dragged up the rear. Oh my gosh! He was wearing a military-style khaki outfit including jodhpurs, jodhpurs boots, puttees, a dress tunic, and cream-colored leather gloves! He was crowned with a beige, wide-brimmed hat. The left side was pinned up as if he were Teddy Roosevelt with the Rough Riders. He was even wearing small gold-rimmed glasses! The Springfield lay across his lap.

They all dismounted except for Mr. Whipple. Dirty Bill was pointing out the burn areas. Major Bohannan was animated, holding his arms out wide like he was on a crucifix. Apparently, he was agitated to learn that the burned-out hulks were missing. Dirty Bill was pointing to wagon tracks headed towards the road to Mr. Mac's spread. The rest of the men looked on in silence.

What happened next took Jack by surprise. Apparently Major Bohannan called a smoke break to give him time to consult with the political member of his staff. The men lit up and walked around stretching their legs.

Dirty Bill began walking briskly, making a beeline straight for Jack. Jack couldn't believe he'd been spotted! He whispered urgently, "I wish I were a copperhead snake for ten minutes." Poof! He was a typical three-feet-long, copper-and-chestnut, brown-banded, triangular-headed, poisonous pit viper coiled up as if to strike.

Dirty Bill stopped to within five feet of Jack. He leaned his shotgun next to a birch tree. He unbuttoned his fly, hauled out his organ, and began to water the ground in the general vicinity of Jack. Suddenly Dirty Bill screamed and jumped as if he had seen a snake! He twisted and reached for his shotgun with his empty hand.

Jack waited nary a second longer. He uncoiled and struck. He bit Dirty Bill right on the tip of what he was holding in his other hand and chomped down as if his life depended on it, because it did. He didn't disengage until every last drop of venom had been injected. Then he let go and began slithering lickety-split back towards Tulip. Militarily, Jack did not consider this a retreat. He considered it a tactical retrograde movement.

Dirty Bill howled like a gut-shot Comanche, staggering around like he was in agony, which he probably was, before he finally collapsed in a heap on the ground. All the men except for Rough Rider Whipple came running to his aid, weapons drawn. Dirty Bill was writhing around screaming, "Shoot it! Shoot it! A copperhead bit my (manhood) on the tenderest part! I'm ruint for life! Maybe even kilt! Oh, dear God, please help me!"

Major Bohannan leaned over and said, "Move your hand. Let me see." He didn't need but a few seconds. He said, "He bit you good. Looks like you got the full dose. It's swelling up and turning dark. The only thing I know to do is tie it off with a shoestring or something to keep the poison from moving up your body to your heart or your brain. If we don't, you'll probably die. If we do, you probably will be ruint forever. I'm so sorry. What would you have us to do?"

"Oh, dear Lord! I'm done for! It hurts somethin' awful. Oh, sweet Jesus! Major, Doc Atkinson only lives three or four miles up the road here towards the Ashland service station. In fact, he's the last house on the right before you get to it. He's got the brick, two-story house. It's my onliest chance. Could you have someone take me there?"

"Of course. Clayton, would you take care of that?"

"You bet."

"Oh, thank you! Thank you!"

"Clayton, when you get done, you might as well meet us back at the camp unless you want to try and meet us at our quarry's cabin. If we're not there yet wait for us out by the road."

"Yes, Sir. Will do. Either way it goes, I'll meet you at the camp by dark."

Beau asked, "Major, why don't you send Mr. Whipple instead of Clay. He's a much steadier hand. Look! That chubby cream puff hasn't even dismounted yet. He looks a little peaked to me like he's fixin' to faint."

The major responded, "Beau and the rest of you all listen up. C.K. Whipple is ready to sell us all down the river if this doesn't go our way. I'm stuck with him. You all know why. If things get bloody, he's gonna get bloody with us. In other words, I'd rather have him inside our tent peeing out, than outside peeing in. Am I clear?"

All four men nodded. The consent was unanimous.

Before Dirty Bill got delirious, the Major asked, "Bill, one last thing. Where do you think the still is located?"

"Continue east. Less than a mile afore you get to MacEwen's property but you'll never know. It's not marked. Look for the Blue Lick Creek. It meanders back and forth but it's southeast of you now. He has to have water to make whiskey. Follow the creek. Look for a hose goin' away from it. The still will be at the end of the hose less'n he's lazy and just sets up by the creek. If'n he's gettin' ready to run a batch, you'll prob'ly smell it afore you see it."

"Thank you. God speed."

Jack didn't hear any of that. By the time the posse started searching for the still, Jack was his human self again, mounted on Tulip, and taking a powder to Gerard's corral.

Chapter 22:
At the End of the Day

Jack stabled Tulip in her stall but left her saddled just in case he needed to skedaddle. As a bonus he gave her a feedbag of oats in addition to the hay in her feed trough. Then he picked up his shotgun and walked up to the verandah where both Gerard and Mr. Mac were smoking and waiting patiently.

Gerard asked, "Ya hungry?"

"Yep. I didn't eat this morning."

"Come on in. I'll fix ya some pancakes and bacon while ya fill us in."

"That sounds great."

They traipsed inside. Jack and Mr. Mac sat down at the table. Gerard poured everyone a cup of coffee. Then he commenced to frying bacon and making pancakes.

Jack said, "I posted up before dawn just east of the demolition site. The posse showed up about two hours later. Dirty Bill was the scout."

Mr. Mac burst out, "Aha! Daggummit! There's your weaselly, stinkin', cow patty-eatin', lowdown snitch! We should 'ave knowed it was him doin' his dirt again. He never learnt the lesson you teached him."

Gerard exclaimed, "What? I wish I had knowed he sneaked back home. I swear I would 'ave broke all his ribs and cut out his tongue!"

Jack responded, "No need. He had a bit of misfortune this morning."

Gerard said, "I didn't hear no gunshots."

"Nope. It was much worse. He was making water and a dern copperhead popped up and bit him on his manhood. He was howlin' in agony, floppin' all around. Wouldn't surprise me none to learn they had to cut it off to save his life. He might 'ave even kicked the bucket by now."

Mr. Mac and Cousin Gerard were hooting with laughter. Gerard said, "Well I'll be a cross-eyed coyote! That'll learn him. What happened next?"

"I don't know. I had to scoot. I was so close to Dirty Bill he almost whizzed on me. All of 'em except for Mr. Whipple came runnin' to help Dirty Bill and kill the snake. From what I saw before that, I think Major Bohannan was upset because the blown-up gangster machines were nowhere in sight.

"Oh, yeah. All six of the posse were there. Not sure what they decided to do about Dirty Bill but my guess is they'll go ahead and search the property tryin' to locate the still. I've checked everything three or four times and there's nothin' there to find. Also, with the possible exception of the major, they're all city boys and now their scout is out of commission. They'll probably show up here in a couple of hours. How do you want to handle it once they get here?"

"Jack, you stay in the barn 'til they ride up. Try not to be seen if'n you can just like we done with the gangsters. You're my ace in the hole again. Me and Mr. Mac will meet 'em from the verandah. I'll tell 'em to get off my property.

"Understand, I ain't submittin' to no arrest. I druther be dead. If they say I am, and I see they mean to take me, that'll be the trigger. I'll light 'em up, no more talk bein' necessary. Otherwise, talk is cheap.

"You fellers feel free to join in if'n shots is fired but wait for me to shoot first. That's real important. I druther they back off without no blood bein' shed but it's their call. That's all I can think of. It ain't no complicated matter. Soon as we get done eatin' it'll be time to set up."

The meal was consumed with minimal further conversation. Everything that needed to be said had been said. Each man was consumed in his own thoughts.

Thirty minutes later Jack climbed up in the hayloft and cracked the board window so he could see the side and front of the cabin. He was undecided if he would shoot from this vantage point or come down. It would be maximum effective range from up there and the buckshot would have a wide spread, possibly hitting someone other than his intended target. On the other hand, it afforded concealment and cover that he would not have on the ground. He would wait and see.

Wait they did. More than three hours. The posse arrived quietly in single file from the front gate. Major Bohannan lead. Rough Rider Whipple was next. Beauregard Greathouse was third, followed by Arthur T. Jackson and finally Buster G. Black, who was riding drag. Clayton E. Simpson was not there.

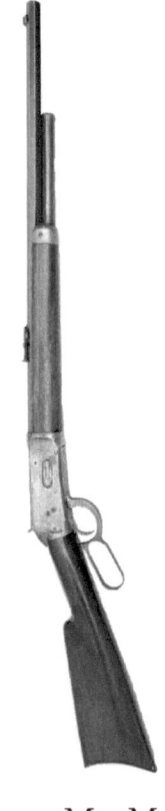

They stopped about twenty feet from the cabin. Major Bohannan was centered directly in front of the steps. C.K. Whipple was to his right. Buster Black was on the right flank. Beauregard Greathouse was to Major Bohannan's left. Arthur T. Jackson was on the left flank nearest to the barn. They sat patiently for two minutes waiting for Gerard to step outside onto the verandah.

Finally, Gerard stepped out, Winchester .30-30 held across his waist in both hands. They could see the hammer was half-cocked. He stood in front of Major Bohannan.

Mr. Mac walked out behind him. He was carrying his Winchester .44-40 in the same fashion. It was half-cocked, too. He stepped to Gerard's left, stopping directly in front of Mr. Whipple, who was holding his Springfield .30-06 across his lap.

Mr. Mac stared at Mr. Whipple, whose Adam's apple was bouncing up and down like a basketball being dribbled by a guard bringing the ball down court across the centerline into play. He was sweating profusely. His eyes were shifting left to right like he was watching a tennis match from the side. Mr. Mac had already sized up the wannabe Rough Rider at the restaurant. He knew Mr. Whipple would never fire a shot. In fact, he would do well to remain in the saddle once shots were exchanged. All Mr. Mac was doing by his stare, was to freeze Mr. Whipple into inaction once bullets began flying. Mission accomplished.

Next, Mr. Mac looked Buster Black in the eye. What he saw was a scared kid with a twelve-gauge pump shotgun. Even so, he saw the kid had grit. He would shoot and at this distance he couldn't miss. It was a shame. Mr. Mac would shoot him first.

Cousin Gerard faced Major Bohannan. So this is what a Medal of Honor winner looks like up close and personal. He was clearly a man who led from the front. He commanded respect. Gerard could see that his Colt .45 was holstered. Nevertheless, he was convinced that the major had a draw like lightning and that he was convinced he could shoot Gerard before Gerard shot him. Brave man.

Gerard gave Beauregard Greathouse a cursory, but respectful glance. Gerard could see both of his Peacemakers which were also holstered. Gerard knew an old-time lawman when he saw one. Gerard knew now without a doubt that he would die, riddled with bullet holes from both Major Bohannan and Mr. Greathouse in the first two seconds of a gunfight. He hoped that Cousin Jack had sized up Mr. Greathouse and that he would eliminate him before he eliminated Gerard, himself. Doubtful.

Finally, he checked out the dandy to his far right. This must be the weasel who shot the kid. He looked cocky. Gerard couldn't see this pimp's gun but he remembered that he carried a pocket pistol in a shoulder holster. Gerard paid him no further thought because for certain, this weasel was a dead man already.

While the antagonists were sizing each other up, Jack quietly descended the ladder and stood in the shadows three feet into the barn. He cocked both barrels. He knew it would be up to him to erase the Wyatt Earp doppelgänger before he erased Gerard. His heart was thumping like a marching band. Nevertheless, he knew what he would do if shots were fired.

The wind was deadly still. The sun was beginning to drop in the west over Buster's shoulder. It was not a factor.

"Mr. Twyman, my name is Major Jubal Bohannan." Looking over at Mr. Mac, he said, "I'm sorry Sir, but I do not know your name although I do remember seeing you in the restaurant Friday eve."

"My name is Elias MacEwen. I am Mr. Twyman's nearest neighbor."

"Of course. Very well. Gentlemen, you know why we're here. We work for the governor's office. We have been commissioned to bring the persons unknown to justice who are responsible for killing nine alleged bootleggers on the Ashland Highway a week ago this past Thursday. In so doing, we are tasked with arresting local moonshiners. Mr. Twyman, we have reliable information that you operate an illegal still and that very likely you were one of the men involved in the killing of the out-of-state bootleggers. What say you, Sir?"

"Major Bohannan, I am honored to meet Kentucky's only living Medal of Honor winner. If you and your men come in peace, I will fix you all a cup of coffee and break bread with you.

"I know who ever'one of you all are. I know your reputations. I know you aren't here to arrest me because Sheriff Harned ain't in your presence. I also know your informant is Wilbur Conard, known far and wide as Dirty Bill, and otherwise known to be an unsavory character of poor reputation - a bald-faced liar. I know he was bitten by a serpent earlier this day. I know you already searched my land and that you couldn't find what ain't there. I am prepared to meet unlawful force with force. If today is my day to die, so be it. Understand that I won't be the onliest casualty here today. I think we understand each other. The next play is yourn."

Jack crept closer to the riders for a definite kill shot on Beauregard Greathouse during Gerard's soliloquy. So far, he had been undetected. When he was within twenty feet, Arthur T. Jackson took his eyes off Mr. Mac, glancing towards the barn. He leapt with a start, crying out, "Ambush!" At the same time, he pulled his revolver and snapped off a hasty, unaimed round at Jack. Jack returned fire and blew him out of the saddle. He was squeezing the trigger to shoot Mr. Greathouse.

Major Bohannan yelled, "Stop! Cease fire, everyone!" His command reverberated throughout the yard. Shockingly, all participants froze in place.

Mr. Whipple's horse apparently didn't understand English. He bucked Mr. Whipple onto the hard-packed earth and galloped off towards the gate.

At least one of Jack's pellets penetrated Mr. Greathouse in his side. He was bleeding. He was also aiming two cocked Peacemakers at Jack.

Buster and Mr. Mac were aiming at each other.

Gerard had shouldered his rifle and was aiming at Major Bohannan, who was sitting in the saddle like he was at a church picnic.

Major Bohannan spoke again, softly. He said, "Please, everyone. Lower your weapons. This is not what I want. Please!"

It seemed like an eternity. First, Gerard lowered his. Then everyone else followed suit.

Major Bohannan said, "Gentlemen, I had misgivings about this mission from the very start. Nevertheless, I followed my orders and everything that's transpired since rests squarely upon my shoulders. I accept the responsibility.

"Mr. Twyman, we will collect our dead and Mr. Whipple, who appears to have broken his arm. Then we're leaving. You, Sir (pointing at Jack), what is your name?"

"My name is John Archibald Rabbit. Folks call me Jack. Gerard is my cousin. I fought with the 1st Infantry Division during the Great War. I live here now."

"Jack, thank you for your service. I can see you are a brave and honorable man. I will tell Judge Durham that you killed Mr. Jackson in self-defense. Maybe we will meet again one day under better circumstances.

"Mr. Twyman, I extend our apologies for coming here today. Same to you, Mr. MacEwen. Before we go, Mr. Twyman, would you mind if we tend to Mr. Greathouse's injuries? Beau, I hope you weren't hit very badly."

"No, Sir. I think I was hit from a spent ball that passed through Mr. Jackson."

Gerard said, "Major, why don't you all dismount and take a breather? Mr. Mac, would you fix the coffee? Jack, why don't you get us some bandages? Fellas, make yourselves to home."

Chapter 23:
Summing Up

That is how the Lawrence County Moonshine War of 1920 ended.

Major Bohannan and the posse returned to Frankfort later that week. Major Bohannan resigned from his job as a bodyguard for the governor. He moved to Louisville and took command of the National Guard's 1st Cavalry Regiment there. The newspapers excoriated Governor Morrow, not him.

C.K. Whipple was unceremoniously fired by his uncle. C.K. found employment as an accountant with the Citizens Fidelity Bank in Lexington. He lived the remainder of his life in obscurity.

Beauregard Greathouse returned to work for the Pinkerton Detective Agency as the operative in charge of the Bowling Green office. He remained highly respected by all who knew him.

Clayton E. Simpson moved back to El Paso. He went back to work at the sheriff's office. Two years later he became the sheriff when Sheriff O'Malley passed away. Clayton was the sheriff for eighteen years.

Buster Black moved to Louisville with Major Bohannan. He was promoted to corporal. He won the Silver Star and a Purple Heart during World War Two. He retired as a master sergeant.

Mr. Mac went back to farming. He lived to be eighty. When he died, he willed all of his land that had belonged to Jack's grandpa back over to Jack.

Gerard continued in the moonshine business even after Prohibition was repealed in 1933, since Lawrence County remained dry until 1941. He married Chloe Arbuckle in 1926. They had four children.

Jack remained at Gerard's for several more years, although he did go visit his sister in North Dakota a month after this final episode of the Lawrence County Moonshine War. He continued to travel off and on until he settled down on Rabbit Hollow years after he received his inheritance. In 1941, he re-enlisted in the Army. He was assigned back to the 1st Infantry Division. He fought in Europe once again.

Neither Gerard, nor anyone else ever knew Jack was a changeling.

The tale wouldn't be complete unless everyone knew what happened to Dirty Bill. He survived, but lost his injured appendage. He was vilified by his family and all the citizens of Lawrence County. He slinked out of town on a southbound L&N train. Years later folks learned he wound up in Sarasota, Florida, where he joined the circus. He became the straw boss for the freak show. Yes, he was a freak, but he never was a performer. He didn't fit in with the freaks, either. In 1924, he was trampled to death by an elephant that he had been abusing.

All's well that ends well.

THE END

About the Author

Earl Snort is the nom de plume of a retired law enforcement officer with more than forty years experience toting a badge and a gun. Before that, he served in the armed forces.

He and his wife have been married fifty years. They reside in the South. They have one son, also a career law enforcement officer, and two grandchildren.

This is the author's fourth foray into the world of writing fiction. After a lifetime of writing non-fiction to document investigations of true crime, he decided to try his hand in make believe.

He hopes you enjoy the yarn.

September 2021

Acknowledgements

The Jack Rabbit concept is the brainstorm of several brilliant individuals with in our publishing environment.

Bruce Moran
Larry Cavanagh
Jeff and Jacki Lovell
Bob Doerr
Linda and Don Brewer
Jessica and Corby Tate
James Thompson
Each of our fantastic Jack Rabbit Fiction Team Writers.

Join me for another
White Glove Fiction adventure
staring Jack Rabbit

www.ingramcontent.com/pod-product-compliance
Lightning Source LLC
Chambersburg PA
CBHW020636110726
47899CB00002B/790